Thug Holiday 2 Christmas Edition

Written by:

Twyla T.

Patrice Balark

Dani Littlepage

J. Dominique

Text <u>ColeHart</u> to <u>42828</u> to be notified of all New Releases!

To stay up to date on new releases, plus get information on contests, sneak peeks, and more, *Click The Link Below...*

http://bit.ly/2BtGCXH

Copyright:

© *Copyright December 2017*

Publisher's Note:

Published by Cole Hart Signature

Dedication:

This book is dedicated to the dopest publisher in the game, Cole Hart!

Salute!!!

Last time in Thug Holiday: Thanksgiving Edition…

Lexi's face was buried inside her phone when she heard the doorbell ring. She thought to herself that maybe Zyree took her up on her offer after all, but her thoughts were confirmed wrong when she heard her family say, "Breeeeee!" in unison. Lexi's eyes slowly raised from her phone just in time to see her best friend/lover walking into the dining room area with a huge smile on her face.

"Heyyyy Bre, we weren't expecting you, but have a seat." Lexi's father said, standing to his feet, greeting Bre.

"It's always a pleasure having you," Mrs. Holiday followed up saying behind her husband.

"Now, wait one damn minute, I ain't get that type of welcome," Aunt Shirley fumed, causing Alyssa's boyfriend Corey to laugh.

Bre went around the table speaking to everyone while purposely skipping Lexi. It was then that Lexi knew that she was on some good bullshit and to prepare herself.

"So Bre, how's school going for you?" Drea asked, handing Bre a dish so she could start making her plate.

"School is going great. I'm looking forward to graduation," Bre spoke while piling turkey, dressing, and macaroni and cheese on her plate.

"Child, you and Lexi sound alike," Mrs. Holiday giggled.

"But, I bet you not breaking your mother's heart by staying away in Atlanta after graduation, are you?" Victoria continued, piercing her eyes at Lexi.

Lexi caught the shade, but instead of acknowledging it, she grabbed her glass to take a sip of her Pepsi.

"Well, Mrs. Holiday, I am actually staying in Atlanta. My girlfriend decided to stay, so I'm staying as well," Bre announced.

Lexi spit out the soda in her mouth as she listened to Bre story about having a girlfriend.

"Uggghhh Lexi, watch what you doing," Drea said, wiping the soda off of her shirt.

"I'm sorry," she apologized while she cut her eyes at Bre.

"Ok wait, so we just gon' sit here and act like this child ain't just admit to having a girlfriend?" Aunt Shirley said, looking around the table at everyone.

"Auntie, it's 2017, you do know gay marriages are legal or are you still stuck in the 60s?" Stasia said, causing her sidekick Lyssa to laugh.

"I know what year it is, but I'm surprised you know about marriages since yours all fucked up," Aunt Shirley shot back, leaving everyone at the table with their mouths wide open.

Lexi was glad that their bickering was taking the spotlight off of Bre, but she was pissed off that she said what she said. Lexi wondered who spilled the beans about her being in Mississippi instead of New York.

"Ok ok ok Shirley, watch your mouth," Abraham warned, pointing his fork in her direction.

"Oh Abraham, shut the hell up. You think that being gay is a sin," Aunt Shirley stated.

"It's in the bible, Shirley. No offense to you, Bre," Mrs. Holiday said, taking up for her husband.

"Victoria be quiet, I know all your secrets from back in the days, so THY SHALL NOT speak about sin," Shirley said, imitating Mr. Holiday's voice.

"Oh my God, ya'll, chill. Let's enjoy this food that's before us," Alyssa said, defusing the situation for the time being.

For a few minutes, there was silence while everyone fed their faces. Lexi prayed to God that the day went as smooth as possible. She wanted to eat and get Bre the fuck out of her parents' house before she said some shit that would result in her getting her ass beat. Chatter began amongst Lexi's parents and her sisters, but she tuned them out. Her mind was everywhere at this moment and for the first time ever, she thought that Bre may actually be crazy enough to tell everyone what was going on between them.

Buzz... Buzz... Buzz... Buzz...

Lexi's phone vibrated on the table several times in a row, indicating that someone was texting her. When she finally looked up from her plate, she noticed Bre smiling at her with a sinister grin. Lexi rolled her eyes before grabbing her phone off the table right after it vibrated again.

"Someone thirsty to talk to you," Anastasia said as she placed more greens on Kyler's plate.

Lexi gave off a fake smile before opening the six unread text messages, all of them from J.R.

J.R.: Wyd

J.R.: When you coming home?

J.R.: Shorty, I think I miss you.

J.R.: You got me texting yo ass like a lame.

J.R.: lol aight I'm done

The fake smile that she gave off a few seconds ago, turned into a real one as she read those messages.

"Well dang, who got you cheesing like that?" Alyssa asked, but before Lexi could reply, Drea yelled out J.R.'s name.

Hearing his name alone caused butterflies to form in her stomach. At first, Lexi thought that she just liked his swag, but as the days went by, she was coming to terms with the fact that she was falling for him.

"And who is J.R.?" Mr. Holiday quizzed.

"He's my friend daddy," Lexi replied, before texting him back and placing her phone back on the table.

"Friend my as--- I mean butt.... J.R. got Baby Holiday nose wide opened," Drea teased.

"Shut up," Lexi snickered, elbowing her oldest sister.

"Well, when are we going to meet this friend?" their mother asked.

"I don't know mommy... I gotta see how it goes," Lexi blushed.

"Well, I can't wait to meet the man that has my baby sis looking all vibrant," Drea beamed, but Lexi heard Bre mumbling.

"Maybe we can meet him soon… what does he do?" Abraham chimed in.

"Oh, you really wanna know what he does?" Bre spoke up and Lexi stared at her, but she wouldn't make eye contact.

She knew that Bre didn't know anything about J.R., so there was no telling what was about to come outta her mouth.

"Bre, are you okay?" Drea quizzed with her head cocked to the side.

"No… I'm not okay. Lexi blew me to the side for this J.R. dude that got her stripping at blue flame.

Before Lexi could stop herself, she stood up and reached across the table and went after Bre, but Drea pulled her back.

"Stripping?" Lyssa and Stasia yelled in unison.

"And what the hell she mean by blew her to the side?" Aunt Shirley added.

"Yeah… y'all precious baby girl and sister is the top stripper at Blue Flame and we've been sleeping together for the past few years until this J.R. nigga popped into the picture!"

"You trifling bitch!" Lexi fumed as she tried to get away from Drea, all to no avail.

"Thanks for dinner, but I'm gonna leave now," Bre said and made her exit.

Lexi heard Alyssa and Anastasia mumbling and snickering, then she turned on them.

"What the fuck y'all snickering about?"

"Alexis Holiday!" Victoria shrieked.

"That's why Lexi my favorite!!" Aunt Shirley cheered.

"Shirley! Stop it… is what she said true, Alexis?" Abraham boomed.

Instead of answering out loud, Lexi fell back into her seat and nodded her head. She couldn't believe that Bre had really just aired her business out in front of her entire family. The thoughts she had running through her head for the next time she laid eyes on her weren't good at all. Her parents were talking, but Lexi tuned them out. She didn't mean to be disrespectful, but she couldn't process the shit that had just happened. She needed a blunt, and she needed one bad. When she stood to leave, her dad's voice made her stop in her tracks, so she had no choice, but to sit down and listen to what he had to say.

***

After all of the drama at dinner the night before, the last thing Anastasia expected was for her family to still want to finish out the weekend. Of course, she didn't mind because for once she wasn't the one being judged. Anastasia felt bad that her baby sister had resorted to such measures to get money, but even worse that she was fucking the girl she had grown up being best friends with. That still wouldn't stop her from throwing jabs every chance she got though. Damn near everything Alexis said she found a way to comment about her being a stripper or being an undercover dyke. Of course, most of the time Andrea intervened, but that didn't stop Anastasia. She had a bone to pick with both of her funny acting sisters, and as soon as the opportunity, she was going to bust Andrea out with the news that Alyssa had given her.

It was surprising that they'd even wanted to continue with their plans to go Black Friday shopping together, but somehow Andrea had managed to get them all to go. They pulled into Walmart's parking lot and Anastasia frowned. She'd already had to ride next to Aunt Shirley's drunk ass, but looking at the store she didn't think they would fair well. For one, the outside was trashed and it wasn't nearly that many people out there. Not that Anastasia wanted to be around a crowd of irritated Americans fighting over scraps, but she knew that if it was empty, then the store was most likely cleaned out. She'd told Andrea that they should have went the night before at 12 like everybody else, but she wasn't trying to hear that.

"What the hell, it ain't even nobody here," Andrea mumbled, looking around before stepping out of her car.

"I told you we should have went last night," Anastasia snipped with an eye roll.

"Shit, we need to leave Walmart anyway, and head to the mall!" Lexi exclaimed. "I know all they sales bussin; especially VS."

"What you tryna go there for, some work clothes?" Anastasia asked with a frown. Lexi looked her way in obvious frustration while Alyssa gave her a high five.

"First off bitch!" she started getting loud and Andrea came to the rescue once again.

"Come on, I been waitin' for yo lil hot ass! Let her go Drea!" Anastasia yelled while Alyssa grabbed her arm to stop her from getting any closer.

"I swear yo ass act like you still in high school, Stasia! Leave this damn girl alone cause we all know damn well you ain't perfect!" Andrea pointed a finger in her face stopping her from struggling against Lyssa. "And Lexi stop letting everything her bitter ass say get to you! You don't have to answer to nobody about what or who you do, especially her," she said, turning to face Lexi. With Drea right there, she calmed down quickly.

"You right big sis... I'm good," Lexi grumbled with her eyes cut in Anastasia's direction.

"That ain't right, Drea. You always taking her side about shit. If it would have been me, both ya'll asses would have been talkin' shit! You always on that favoritism shit I swear," Anastasia fumed, snatching out of Lyssa's hold.

"All ya'll bitches need to shut up! In the parking lot of Walmart ain't the place to be airing this shit out. We all know Alexis is a lil strippin' dyke now and we all know Anastasia ass bitter as hell cause she don't want Richard ole crusty ass! Now, leave that girl alone so we can go on in this store and I can see what deals they got on this liquor up in here!" Aunt Shirley snapped, getting in between them all as she fixed her wig on her head. Anastasia's face twisted up into a frown at her putting her business on front street, but she didn't say anything and neither did Lexi, even though her face held the same irritation. They both knew that there was no arguing with Shirley; especially, when she was drunk, and she had already filled her flask twice that morning. With a satisfied smirk, Andrea looped her arm through Lexi's and walked ahead of them all.

Anastasia and Alyssa shared a look cause they already knew that they were up there talking shit about them.

"Come ya'll asses on! I don't know why ya'll so cliqued up and ya'll all siblings," Aunt Shirley continued to fuss, waving them ahead of her.

With a deep sigh, the two sisters entered the store with their Aunt behind them still going off. Anastasia grabbed a cart hoping that she could at least find something to get Kyler since she knew the early risers had already been all through there. She was glad that he had gone with his father instead of tagging along with them since they hadn't even been alone for an hour and had already gotten into an argument.

"Sis, you know I got yo back," Alyssa whispered to her, so that their Aunt Shirley wouldn't hear. She gave her a sympathetic look and patted her back as they maneuvered through the store to get to the electronic section.

"I know, boo; apparently, you're the only one."

"Stasia, you already know it's been like that. Drea gone always come to Lexi's defense and I'm gone always come to yours, it ain't right, but it's just how shit goes," Lyssa shrugged, grabbing a candle set off the shelf and throwing it in the cart.

"It's still fucked up," Anastasia noted and Alyssa merely nodded. She didn't know when things had turned into a tag team affair whenever the sisters were around each other, but she wasn't about to let this shit with Lexi die down. Like she'd said, if it would have been her who had a secret lesbian affair with her childhood friend and had been shaking her ass in somebody's club for dollars, all hell would have broken loose. She was tired of Lexi always getting off easy and Andrea always taking up for her right

15

or wrong, so until she saw fit, she was gonna bring up the situation every chance she got.

At some point the girls lost their Aunt, but found their sisters in the electronics department. Still a little irritated about the whole argument, Stasia kept a small distance between them as she tried to find Kyler some headphones and games in all of the rubbish. Luckily, she was able to find a few games that were age appropriate and even a couple of movies despite the chaos that had taken place there that morning. She was even able to find Richard a camera and a cute digital picture frame to go in his office. Knowing him, he'd find something to complain about even though she didn't have to bring his ass shit.

"Oh, my God! Anastasia!" Stasia heard her name being called and turned around to see Lizz standing there with a cart and a huge grin. Surprised. she made her way over to her and exchanged air kisses and a hug.

"Hey girl! What you doin down this way?" she wanted to know.

Lizz had never mentioned having family down south and Jackson was the last place anybody would come for vacation, let alone Lizz's stuck up ass.

"Oh, you know the fellas had that damn conference out this way," Lizz chuckled a little bit and looked away.

"Oh duh," Stasia joined her and gave her arm a tap.

Of course, Harold would have to attend the same conference as Richard. They worked closely together and most times you wouldn't see one without the other. She was shocked that Lizz had decided to join him though. Usually, when Harold went out of town, she would leave with her lil boo until he returned, but it was still good to see her nevertheless.

"You here alone?"

"Aw hell yeah! You know Harold's old ass ain't tryna be out going to all these stores." She waved her off with another laugh.

"I know right. It would have been like pulling teeth to get Richard out here." Anastasia rolled her eyes. She could see Alexis and Andrea next to the cd's, but looking in their direction. Figuring that they were talking about her being rude for not introducing them, she sucked her teeth. "Come meet my sister's girl before they say I'm actin' funny."

"Uhh...I was actually about to leave," Lizz trailed off, turning away slightly. "I'll just catch you later."

"Don't be silly, it's only gone take a minute," Anastasia insisted, pulling her over to where her sisters stood. Alyssa made her way towards them at the same time and Stasia went ahead and introduced them all quickly.

"Guys this is my friend, Lizz, from New York, Lizz, these are my sisters Andrea, Alexis, and Alyssa," she said, pointing at each one as she named them. They all waved, but Anastasia noticed Lexi and Drea share a look after they gave her a dry ass hey.

"It's nice to meet you all, but ummm I was on my way out. Harold been blowing me up," she said, looking at her phone like it would ring any minute.

"Well okay, just hit me up. Me and Richard are gonna be here until Sunday night. We should get together before we go back," Stasia drawled, giving her a strange look. She didn't really understand the rush, when she knew that Lizz never did anything when or how Harold wanted.

"Alright, I will," she called over her shoulder as she walked away with her phone to her ear. When she turned back to her sisters, Drea and Lexi were watching Lizz's retreat, before Lexi shrugged and went back to browsing the cd's in her hand.

"Ya'll was just rude as hell," Anastasia tilted her head and looked over to her sisters with knitted brows. "Is that how strippers act when they meet new people?"

"Bitch, you ain't got but one more time to come for me-."

"And what's gone happen? Huh? Not shit!" Stasia damn near shouted lunging in her sister's direction. She was yanked back before she could get too close, while Drea put an arm up to hold Lexi back.

"Ughhhhhh! I swear you talk so much fuckin' shit bitch and yo shit ain't nowhere near as perfect as you think!" Lexi shouted trying to get around Drea.

"Don't do this shit here, Alexis!" Andrea hissed, struggling with Lexi.

"So, what hoe? We all know that I ain't happy with Richard, sooooo what? At least I got a man and ain't out here dancing for dollars and getting' fucked with a strap on!"

"We don't use a strap you dumb ass hoe! I ride that hoe face just like that bitch that just left rides Richard's!" Lexi snapped, clapping her hands after each word. Shocked, Anastasia stopped fighting against Alyssa and blinked confused.

"What the fuck you talkin' bout, Lexi?" She wanted to know, now trying to get around Andrea who was looking defeated.

"I'm sayin that your "husband" been fuckin' yo so-called friend dummy! That's what she doin' out here!"

"I told you not to bring that shit up here, Lexi, damn!" Andrea sighed loudly, throwing her head back.

"Oh, so you knew about this shit too, Drea? And ya'll bitches wasn't gone say shit?" Anastasia let out a bitter laugh and shook off Lyssa as she tried to wrap her arms around her shoulders.

"I swear I just found out when ole girl walked up," Drea turned to face her with both hands up in defense.

"Right and ya'll lettin' me sit here and Keke with this hoe and didn't say shit?" she asked with a trembling voice. "Ya'll want to see me hurt that bad, huh?"

"Oh, bitch please! First of all, you don't even want that nigga, and secondly, you been throwing shots at me like a muthafucka, now you want to sit and act like you soooo hurt! Miss me with that shit. Shouldn't have allowed your husband to stay at a fuckin hotel without you. That's where I saw em at," Lexi smacked her lips and waved Stasia off.

"That shit still ain't cool, Lexi, and you know it! Real shit, ya'll should have said somethin' and we all was sposed to get in that hoe ass regardless," Alyssa finally spoke and for the first time, Stasia thought about the fact that Lizz's hoe ass might possibly still be there.

Without saying a word, she took off running back towards the front of the store in search of that pale bitch.

She scanned the lines and saw that she wasn't at any of the registers before rushing out the automatic doors with Alyssa calling her back.

"Ahhhh!" she yelled loudly as she looked through the lot for any sign of that bitch. Anastasia knew she was long gone, but she wouldn't stop walking through the parking lot.

"Anastasia, calm down!" Alyssa yelled, grabbing ahold of her arm so that she couldn't continue to walk up on cars.

"Calm down? You want me to calm down when this lame ass nigga been fuckin' my so-called friend behind my back?"

"Yes Stasia! Be real with yourself, you don't even really care! This is a way for you to get out of your marriage easy! Can't you see that!" she pleaded, but Anastasia wasn't trying to hear any of that shit. Regardless of if she wanted to be with Richard or not, she was still pissed that he had the audacity to fuck someone else, let alone someone she called a friend. Sure, she had her someone on the side, but at least he didn't know the person. He had that bitch in her face day in and day out like it was okay.

"You think I give a fuck! We all know this shit wasn't about love!" Anastasia shouted with her arms spread. "This shit is about respect! Off GP that bitch was off limits!" she didn't care that there were people standing there watching her act a fool, she didn't care about anything at that moment, but getting at that bitch for disrespecting her and fucking Richard up.

"Stasia, calm yo ass down out here givin these white folks a show!" Aunt Shirley came out of nowhere shuffling across the parking lot with a bag in one hand and her flask in the other. "Gone on about ya'll business! Out here being nosey and shit like ya'll don't be fuckin ya'll cousins, brothers and sisters! Ole inbred asses!" she growled, waving off the group of bystanders that were standing there. They all walked off slowly knowing that they didn't want any problems with the loud mouth lady in the blue dress.

"Naw, right now ain't the time, Aunt Shirley!"

"You think I give a damn about what time it is girl? You out here showin' yo natural black ass and for what?"

"Oh, you don't know! It seems my damn husband has been fuckin' my friend and nobody bothered to tell me!" she said, slapping a hand against her chest angrily.

"Aw girl please, anybody with half a damn brain can tell that Richard cheating on yo ass fool! You think that man don't know you ain't happy? I know yo ass ain't doing shit wifely, so of course he was gone find somebody to fulfill those needs! You feel that highly of yourself that you don't think he would want anybody but you?" Aunt Shirley asked, instantly shutting her up.

"I ain't tryna hear that shit right now, Aunty," Anastasia shook her head fighting the truth of her words.

"Oh, so you cursing me, now? Huh? Yo ass ain't that mad and you damn sure ain't too grown for me to whoop yo yellow ass!"

Anastasia was so mad that her vision was blurry and the last thing she wanted was to sit and listen to her Aunty go in on her when she wasn't the one in the wrong, well to their knowledge anyway. Where the fuck was she when Alexis had put her business out there inside of a damn

21

Walmart? She blew a frustrated breath and closed her eyes as she tried to gather her thoughts.

"Stasia, let's just get out of here," Alyssa suggested, wrapping her arms around her sister. "I already set up an Uber," she let her know as Anastasia fell into her embrace while she rubbed her back.

It didn't even take the Uber five minutes to get there, letting Anastasia know that her sister had been setting up the ride while she had her meltdown. Lyssa always knew what to do and when to do it and in that moment, she was happy to have at least one of her sisters in her corner. They both climbed inside of the awaiting car and Anastasia couldn't wait to get home, so that she could fuck Richard up. She watched her sisters come out of the store and meet their Aunt at the car before they pulled away.

***

As soon as the car drove off, Anastasia was on her phone calling Richard's punk ass. He ignored her the first time, but picked up on the first ring the second time.

"Hello?" he answered and she could hear the hesitation in his voice because she never really called him for anything.

"Where the fuck you at Richard?"

"I'm at the house…. why?" he questioned, sounding nervous.

"Cause I just ran into yo lil hoe, Lizz, at Walmart nigga!" she snapped. "I'ma fuck you and her up, so stay yo ass right there!" she continued as the line went silent.

Pulling the phone away from her ear, she realized that the nigga had hung up on her. "Oh no the fuck he didn't!"

"What?"

"That pussy ass nigga hung up on me!" Stasia vented furiously as she attempted to call him back. Of course, he kept sending her ass to voicemail, but that didn't stop her from calling.

"What did you call him for? You should have just popped up on his ass and started fuckin him up, now he know and he probably gone be gone by the time we get there," Lyssa commented rolling her eyes.

"Oh, he bouta catch this fade! It ain't nowhere he can run that I won't find his ass!" she couldn't believe that he had done something so low down.

How long had they been fucking around? When had it started? Was that hoe telling him her business? Did he know about D'Mani? Those were all the questions running through her mind as the car cruised back to her parent's house. She knew that they were both unhappy, and yeah, she might have felt like Richard wouldn't cheat on her, but a small part of her knew that something was going on. Her friend though? That was the last person she expected for him to have been having an affair with. Richard was just like Lizz's husband, Harold, only younger. What in the hell had made her want to talk to the black version of her husband? The way that she'd talked about him had made it seem as if he was laid back and down to earth, the total opposite of Richard. Anastasia wondered if maybe he had just been putting on a show for her benefit this whole time and really wasn't as uptight as he made himself out to be.

"I'm still stuck on the fact that them hoe ass sisters of ours didn't say shit!" Alyssa vented.

"Like you said, Drea and Lexi always gone have each other backs and we gone do the same," Stasia said shaking her head.

She had a problem with her sisters too for keeping some information like that away from her. It seemed like they had planned on not telling her and probably laughing about it behind her back.

"If that's how you see it," Alyssa mumbled with an eye roll as the car pulled up to the house. Anastasia noticed that Richard's rental wasn't parked out front, but that didn't stop her from jumping out of the car and speed walking into the house ready to get into Richard's ass.

She stormed through the house and looked for him getting pissed off as she came up empty. She should have known his ass was gone try and leave when she mentioned Lizz's hoe ass. It would have been smarter to have done what Lyssa had said and just popped up on his ass. She ran back down the stairs to see her standing in the living room as Drea, Lexi, and Aunt Shirley all filed into the front door.

"Where the hell that nigga at!" Aunt Shirley asked, looking around the living room.

"He's gone already," Alyssa explained, glancing in her direction. They all stepped further inside of the house and Anastasia noticed that both of her sisters had sour looks on their faces.

"You must have called him before you got here?" Andrea observed.

"Why do you even care, bitch? Yo ass wasn't worried about me earlier," Anastasia watched as Drea closed her eyes and took a deep breath like she was getting on her nerves.

"Anastasia, what you ain't gone do is act like it's my fault yo husband was fuckin yo friend! You know damn well if we would have told you, you wouldn't have believed shit we said, so cut it the fuck out!" Andrea called her out.

"Preach!" Alexis spoke up from on the side of her.

"That's not true!" Anastasia tried to lie.

She knew that if they would have brought that information to her before they had run into Lizz, she would have never believed it. It wasn't like they had the best relationship, so there would have been no reason for her to believe that they were telling her the truth.

"Listen, I'm not about to argue with you, Stasia. You know what I'm saying is true. Regardless of what you may think of us though, we do love you and we weren't trying to keep it away from you to hurt you. I wanted to figure out the best way to approach the situation, because at Walmart this morning wasn't the time or place."

"Listen to yo damn sister for once and stop being so fuckin stubborn!" Aunt Shirley scolded from her spot on the couch.

"Ya'll need to put ya'll differences aside for the time being and go whoop Richard's ass together!" she exclaimed.

The sister's all looked around, each considering what their Aunt was saying. They all knew that even though they'd had their issues in the past they always put them aside to band together when the situation called for it. Those moments were few and far between, but they had happened and now was one of those times.

Anastasia's phone vibrated in her hand and she unlocked the screen to see a text from Richard.

Richard: I left Kyler there with your mother and went back to the hotel. I don't have time to argue with you about your crazy assumptions, Ana.

Anastasia: Oh, you can text, but yo bitch ass can't answer the phone, huh?

She waited for a reply, but it never came and she knew he saw it because his read receipts were on. That nigga was really trying to turn this shit around on her like she was crazy or some shit. For as stuck up as Richard wa,s he was doing typical hood nigga shit and Anastasia was not standing for it.

"Uggghh I'ma fuck him up!" she shrieked loudl,y stopping the conversation that was going on around her.

"What?" Lyssa asked with her brows knitted together and everyone's eyes landed on Anastasia.

"That nigga just texted and said he left Kyler with mama and he's gone cause he ain't tryna argue with me about my crazy assumptions!"

"His ass know damn well," Alexis sucked her teeth.

"He think he slick! He know I don't know what hotel his ass is in."

"Well, I do and I know what room he in," Alexis let it be known with both hands on her hips. A hush fell over the room.

"Ya'll bitches tryna do a Holiday sister beat down or nah?"

"I'm with it," Andrea shrugged and began to tie back her hair.

"You already know I'm comin," Lyssa chimed in.

"Yessss, that's what I'm talkin' bout! Now, let's go!" Aunt Shirley exclaimed as she popped up from the couch.

Anastasia immediately started shaking her head no.

"Hell, naw, Aunty! You too old to be tryna fight anybody. You stay here," she said, causing their Aunt to smack her lips.

"Who you callin' old? I can twerp this booty and knock a hoe out just like ya'll can, shit!"

"First of all, it's twerk, Aunt Shirley," Andrea sighed and pinched the bridge of her nose while Lexi laughed.

"Shiiiit, I say we bring her," Lexi said with a wide grin.

"Ya'll wastin' all this time and I'm comin' no matter what! Now, let's go before that tight booty ass nigga of hers leave and I have to catch a flight!" Aunt Shirley snapped, walking past all of them and out of the front door. Alexis was the first one to follow behind her, then Andrea went out right after. Anastasia let out a heavy sigh and motioned for Alyssa to follow her, and they both filed out after their sisters, locking the door behind them.

When they pulled up at the Residence Inn thirty minutes later, Anastasia turned up her nose at the thought of them having been there fucking the whole time. Even though she had done her dirt somehow, she still felt betrayed by finding out that Richard was cheating. Maybe it was because it was a blow to her confidence. Anastasia never thought that he would cheat on her, especially not with someone she considered a friend. She real life was blind-sided by this whole thing and even worse, it had all come out in front of her sisters.

"Oh, he got this hoe in a nice lil hotel, huh? He a damn dummy, all real niggas know that you take yo side hoe to a cheap ass hotel; that's what they named for Hoe! Tell!" Aunt Shirley started going off as soon as Andrea put the car in park. She damn near knocked Anastasia down trying to get out.

"What room they in, Lexi?" Andrea asked their little sister as soon as they all were out of the car.

"I saw them go in room 308. That's on the third floor," she told them before heading inside without waiting.

They each walked past the front desk not worried about being stopped, but they could easily just say that Anastasia was trying to surprise her husband. Luckily, there was no one behind the desk when they came in, so they all filed inside of the elevator.

"Oooh, I can't wait to beat this nigga ass!" Lexi fumed, watching the numbers go up.

"Calm yo ass down, Lexi; this Stasia fight," Andrea said, causing Lexi to give her a crazy look.

"Now, you know Anastasia ass ain't gone want no parts in this for real…"

"Oh, naw this all me, ya'll," Anastasia cut her off just as the bell dinged and the doors slid open.

Alexis tried to beat her sisters off of the elevator, but Anastasia managed to get through the doors first. She

28

stormed down the halls checking the numbers on each door until she found Richard's. With a raised hand, she prepared herself to knock on the door when Alyssa grabbed her arm to stop her.

"Bitch, if he see you at this door he ain't gone open it," she hissed in a whisper in case he could hear them on the other side of the door.

"Shit," Anastasia mumbled because she hadn't thought about that, but before they could come up with a plan, Aunt Shirley pushed her way through them and knocked on the door covering the peephole with a finger. They all looked at her in shock, not sure of what she was going to say.

"Naw, Aunt Shirley..." Andrea began, but Aunt Shirley waved her off and told her to shut her ass up. With a frown, she pursed her lips together and folded her arms.

"Who is it?" Rich's voice broke through the silence that followed and Aunt Shirley cleared her throat.

"Room service," she slurred in what was supposed to be a Spanish accent, but it came out sounding like she was a cartoon character. They all fought to hold in the laughter that threatened to come out from her attempt at disguising her voice.

"I didn't order anything from room service," he grumbled as he opened the door with his head down. As soon as there was enough space to fit through, Alexis threw a jab that landed right on his nose causing it to leak.

"What the fuck?"

"Yeah nigga! You thought you was gone get away with playin my sister, huh?" Alexis shouted, pushing her way inside the room as Richard tried to close the door on them. She landed another blow to his face knocking him on his ass and they all filed inside of the room.

"Bitch, I told you I wanted to hit his ass first!" Anastasia said, sucking her teeth. She grilled Lexi who now stood over Richard and shrugged with a smile.

"Shit, I was just warming him up for you."

"I'm going to call the police!" Richard cried from his spot on the floor with his hand over his nose.

"You ain't callin shit, bitch!" Lexi ranted and kicked in his direction.

"I knew his ass was a pussy!" Anastasia heard her Aunt say from behind her.

"Oh yes, the hell I am! Ana, why would you bring your sister's here to try and fight me?" he wanted to know.

"Shut up! You don't get to ask her no questions," Andrea who was standing behind him now spat and slapped him on the back of the head.

"Fuck him up, Stasia!"

Anastasia stepped closer to him and was now standing between his legs. She squatted in his face and slapped the cowboy shit out of him. She laughed at how he dramatically grabbed the side of his face and looked up at her in fear.

"You know you got some nerve to be cheating on me with that bitch, Lizz!" she said through clenched teeth. "All this time, I been trying to stick it out with you, and you go and do this!" She went to hit him again, but paused as he began to laugh.

"Really Anastasia? I got some nerve when you've been fucking a low life thug behind my back for how long?" he asked with a bitter laugh as her eyes widened in shock. "Oh, you didn't think I knew, huh?

"This ain't about her! This about your low-down ass. Shit, I'd be fuckin a thug too if I had to sleep next to yo boring ass every night!" Lexi scoffed from the side.

"Shit, ain't that the truth! He don't even look like he got good dick, hell! I ain't even got my glasses on and I can see that," Aunt Shirley chimed in and all eyes landed on her. Of course, she had her flask out and Anastasia shook her head at her Aunt who merely shrugged and took another sip.

"Anyway," Stasia dragged. "That's not the same thing, Richard! That was my friend! You introduced us!"

"Speakin of which, where that hoe at?" Alyssa questioned, looking around as if she would just appear out of nowhere.

"Hell yeah, that's what I wanna know!" Andrea added.

"Why are they even here, Ana, damn!"

"Bitch, don't question us! We here to beat yo ass!" Richard looked up at Lexi and rolled his eyes.

"You just showin yo ass cussin and bragging on fuckin that hoe to me, huh?" Anastasia tilted her head and gave him a sinister grin. She really didn't even know how she had put up with his shit all of this time for fear that D'Mani would play her out when her safety net had been doing it all along.

"Look Ana, I don't know what you want me to say. I'm confused on why you're even so upset when you don't even want to be with me. The only thing keeping us together is my son at this point and you know it," he tried to reason with her as he wiped the small trickle of blood from his lip. She couldn't even lie and say that she didn't understand his point, because what he was saying was true. There were no feelings there, but she still felt betrayed by him and the bitch that she had considered a friend. To top that off, she had wasted so much time pushing D'Mani away for him and she might have lost him forever when her own husband had been fucking around on her.

"Don't try and turn this shit around on her, nigga!" Lyssa said sucking her teeth. "Don't nobody got no sympathy for you."

"Where is she?" was all Stasia wanted to know at this point.

They had gotten their round with him and now, it was Lizz's turn. There was no way that she could allow that hoe to get off scott free, she was most definitely catching a fade. He shook his head and mumbled something under his breath that she couldn't make out.

"You think this shit is a game? Where that hoe at?" Alexis yelled and tried to get at him, but Andrea held her back.

"I honestly don't know and I wouldn't tell you anyway, fuckin' bitch!" he said with narrowed eyes.

"See, I was tryna save yo ass!" Andrea said and let Lexi go. As soon as she was free, she ran over and they all started kicking him as he wailed in pain. Even Aunt Shirley went over and threw in a few licks with her purse. They were all digging in his ass until a pounding at the door stopped them. Richard rolled around on the floor moaning in pain and Lyssa squatted in his face and slapped him.

"Shut up, bitch boy."

"Security! Open this door!" They all heard from the other side and their eyes widened in surprise.

"Oh, shit ya'll I'm on probation! I can't be goin back to jail!" Aunt Shirley whispered, taking a long gulp of her drink. She started mumbling to herself and they all looked at her like she was crazy.

"What is you doin?"

"Shit, I'm prayin'. God gotta come through!"

"Lawd Aunty, chill out. I got this," Alyssa sighed and stood up, straightening out her clothes before heading to the door.

"Wait bitch, don't open that!" Lexi hissed, but Lyssa waved her off and went to open the door.

Two beefy security guards stood on the other side with scowls on their faces. Thankfully they couldn't see Richard from where they stood, and Lexi stood right next to him and threatened to fuck him up if he made a sound.

"May I help you gentlemen?" Alyssa asked with a smile on her face. The two guys looked her over, then their eyes swept the room before coming back to her.

"Yes, we've been receiving calls about yelling and screams coming from this room." The biggest of the two said stepping closer, but she put a hand up to stop him.

"Sorry about that fellas," she said and pulled out her badge.

"I got a fugitive in here and he was putting up a little bit of a fight, but me and my associates have it under control."

The two men eyed her badge, then looked around the room again at all of the sisters since Aunt Shirley had moved behind the wall with Alexis and Richard. The one who spoke first nodded his head in understanding, then backed up a little. "FBI huh? How about you let me take you out sometime, cause I ain't never seen an agent that looked like you." He tried his luck at flirting and Anastasia immediately let out a sigh of relief. If he was trying to flirt with Alyssa that meant that they didn't see them as a threat.

"Sorry honey, but I'm engaged," she told him, flashing her ring. "But, the bureau appreciates your fast response." With that, she closed the door in his face. When she turned back around to face her sisters, Andrea was giving her a slow clap while Stasia and Lexi were laughing their asses off.

"Damn, that was close girl. I'm glad you had your badge on you," Drea said beaming.

"Nah, fuck all that! Bitch, you the jakes?" Aunt Shirley gasped.

"Yes, Aunt Shirley, I work for the FBI," Lyssa replied with an eye roll.

"That's some shit you need to disclose before I come around, girl; ain't no tellin' what I might have confessed to around yo ass," she fussed.

"Look, we done beat his ass and almost got caught, let's just go before anything else happen," Andrea suggested and they all agreed.

"Hell yeah, I made my point already," Lexi trilled and flipped her hair over her shoulder.

"Okay, but before we go." Alyssa stopped them and pulled her gun out of her purse pointing it in Richard's face.

"You are not to tell anyone about this, understood?" she coaxed and with his nose turned up, Richard nodded his understanding.

"Okay Richard, I'm giving you a chance here. I would hate for my nephew to lose his daddy because you made the dumb decision to lie to me." She stared him down for a few more seconds before popping up to her feet and tucking her gun away.

"Now, we can go ya'll." She shrugged while they all stared at her in surprise. Well, all except Lexi who had a wide grin on her face.

"Yo, that shit was gangsta as hell!" she gushed. "I gotta get me one of them lil bitches."

"Hell yeah, me, too!" Aunt Shirley added as they both walked past Richard and she smacked him upside the head with her purse. Shaking her head, Andrea followed them out with Alyssa right behind her.

Anastasia looked down at the man that she'd spent the last few years of her life with as he wiped at his nose since it wouldn't stop bleeding. With a shake of her head, she stepped around him.

"Good bye, Richard," she said with her head held high as she walked away.

"Oh, and I want a fucking divorce!" Were her last words as she slammed the door shut on him and their marriage.

***

A knock on her bedroom door woke Alyssa up the next morning. She didn't know what time it was, but after the crazy evening she had endured with her sisters and Aunt, she wasn't ready to welcome the new day yet. Tossing the covers off her, she dragged herself out of bed and over to the door. She opened the door halfway and saw her dad standing on the other side.

"Good morning, sleepy head," he said with a chipper tone.

"Hey Dad! What's going on?" Alyssa asked in a groggy tone.

"I just came back from getting the Christmas tree and I need that fiancé of yours to help me bring the decorations out of the basement. So, hurry and get yourself together."

"What time is it?"

"Almost eleven. I woke your sisters up, too. So, don't think I'm just picking with you," he chuckled.

"Okay, Dad. We'll be down in a minute." She closed the door and grabbed her suitcase looking for something to wear. After picking out her outfit, Alyssa woke Corey up with a light shake.

"I'm up, Lyssa and I know your father wants me to help him bring the decorations up from the basement."

"Well, get your ass up and get ready." She hit him playfully in his head.

"I'm surprised you're still here. I thought you would've been on the first plane out of here after what happened a couple days ago."

"I ain't gonna lie. Ya family definitely got some issues, bae, but that's not enough to scare me away. Ya Aunt Shirley is crazy as fuck though," he chuckled.

"Who you telling?" She shook her head.

Alyssa watched as Corey got out of bed and threw on a tee shirt over his wife beater and a pair of pajama pants. It had been a while since she had some dick and wanted to fuck him badly, but she couldn't bring herself to fuck him in her parents' house. They shared a quick kiss before they walked out the room heading in different directions. Alyssa walked to the bathroom and handled her hygiene before getting dressed for the day.

A little while later, she walked downstairs where she found her dad, sisters, nephew, and Corey in the living sorting through decorations, while her mother and Aunt Shirley were cooking in the kitchen. Alyssa greeted all her sisters and nephew with hugs before helping with the decorations. For the first time since she arrived, Alyssa was at ease with spending time with her sisters. Whooping Richards' ass the night before seemed to bring them closer and for the first time since she arrived, the tension was gone. Alyssa couldn't recall when the relationship with her sisters became so strain, but it felt good to bond with them.

After they sorted through all the decorations, Alyssa and Andrea began decorating the living room while Alexis, Anastasia, and Kyler decorated the tree. Victoria and Aunt Shirley made everyone take a lunch break and as soon as they were finished, they went back to decorating and everyone gathered in the living room. The laughter, talking and joking added to the peaceful atmosphere as they finished decorating the house.

Around five that evening, Alexis and Anastasia went into the kitchen to help their mother warm up the leftover Thanksgiving food while everyone else hung out in the living room. Alyssa sat next to Corey on the couch and Aunt Shirley was sitting next to Alyssa with her flask in hand. Their dad sat comfortably in his favorite chair while Andrea was posted up in the doorway. Abraham was in control of the TV and when he turned to the news, they sat quietly and watched. A few minutes later, a story about an innocent young black man who they portrayed as a thug being gunned down by white cops in a case of mistaken identity caught everyone's attention. Aunt Shirley nudged Alyssa to get her attention and nodded her head in her fathers' direction. Alyssa saw how upset he was and before she could ask what was wrong, her father spoke.

"These freaking cops make me sick. They're always so quick to gun down the innocent. They don't care if they have their facts straight or not. All they care about is that they got another black man off the streets. Didn't help me to see this on the day of my brother's death anniversary," he fumed.

"Daddy, don't tell me you still have ill feelings towards that cop," Alyssa asked in disbelief.

"After they shot and killed my twin brother because of mistaken identity, you damn right I do! My brother was an upstanding citizen, not the thug they wanted him to be and think all blacks are!" he stared at her. "Cops don't give a damn about no one, except for their own kind. The officer that killed my brother didn't lose his badge or serve any jail time. Everyone in law enforcement are a bunch of pigs. Including the black people that work in that field," he boomed.

Alyssa looked around the room and all eyes were on her except for her fathers'.

"I know that it must hurt dad, but you can't blame all law enforcement for the mistake one man made."

"Alyssa, you gonna just sit there and act like you don't know the pain it caused? How dare you... all cops can go to hell if you ask me!

"So, I guess I'm going to hell? Huh, Dad?"

"What?" he looked at her again.

"I'm an FBI agent, Daddy. So, that makes me a pig too? And it means I'm going to jail?"

Abraham stood to his feet and so did Alyssa. They met each other in the middle of the floor and stared at each other for a minute. Everyone had gathered into the living room, but the room was so quiet you could hear a mouse piss on cotton.

"Aww shit, now. This gonna be a good one right here! But wait... Lyssa you better remember I'm your aunt. I got warrants and shit, but you better stay the hell away from me!" Aunt Shirley cackled as she took a drink from her flask.

"Please tell me that you're joking, Alyssa," Abraham winced.

"No, I'm not. I've been an agent for a couple of months now."

"Well you need to call and tell them that you resigned," he demanded.

"I will do no such thing. I like what I do and I will not quit my job because of your ill feelings towards law enforcement. What happened to our uncle was unfortunate, but it happened years ago. You need to learn how to forgive and let it go, Dad."

"I will never forgive them for what they did to my brother," he boomed.

"Abraham, you're so full of shit. How the hell are you preachin' every Sunday and tellin' your congregation to be like Christ and you're doin' the complete opposite? Jesus forgives people for their sins and you're not able to forgive the people who took your brother's life. You're a hypocrite," Aunt Shirley lashed out.

"I'm surprised you know anything about Christ at all, Shirley," Abraham stated harshly.

"I know that He turned water to wine and I am forever greatly to Him for that. Cheers," Aunt Shirley lifted her flask before taking it to the head.

"Aunt Shirley is right, Dad, and you know it."

"I'm willing to forgive people for certain things, but I'll never forgive the bastards that took my brother's life, but I'm willing to forgive you for joining the FBI if you're willing to quit."

"I already told you, Dad. I'm not quitting my job and as far as I'm concerned, you need to quit being a pastor because you're not living what you're preaching."

"Wait a minute, Alyssa. I know that you're upset with daddy, but I will not stand here and let you disrespect him," Andrea jumped in.

"Excuse me?" Alyssa walked over to her.

"Don't tell Dad he needs to quit being a pastor. What he preaches about helps people in their everyday lives and lets them know that they can turn to Christ for all their needs, worries and concerns. No man is perfect, but daddy is damn near perfect and let's not forget everything he's done for us. You better watch your tone," Andrea stated confidently.

"You've got to be fucking kidding me, Andrea. Do you hear yourself right now? I understand that forgiving someone is not an easy thing to do, but if my pastor isn't taking his own advice when it comes to his personal life, why the hell should someone else follow his advice?"

"You knew that daddy was going to have a problem with you being a FBI agent. That's why you kept it from us for so long. We constantly tried to keep up with you and find out what you had going on. You should have been woman enough to tell us instead of keeping it a big secret. It's not just daddy that don't like cops, you see how many innocent blacks those bastards keep killing!"

"I can't believe you're really standing here defending him right now. For your information, I kept it from y'all because I knew y'all wouldn't support me, but I never thought it would be behind some shit that happened years ago. Unlike you Andrea, I'm not afraid to live my life. I'm a grown as woman and I will live my life the way I choose to. I'm not going to let our parents' run my life like they run yours."

"Andrea is living her life like she's supposed to. Our guidance is the reason that she doesn't have any children out of wedlock like most of these young people these days. Andrea is a very successful woman and unlike you, Alyssa, she wouldn't do nothing to deliberately hurt her father."

"I didn't do anything to you Dad, but you will be hurt by someone's careless actions sooner than later."

"Noooo you didn't just say that!" Aunt Shirley shrieked.

Andrea balled up her fists and stepped towards Alyssa, but Corey walked up and grabbed Alyssa by the arm and ushered her out of the living room. Alyssa looked up and saw that her mother, Alexis, and Anastasia was watching everything from the kitchen. Instead of continuing the conversation, she didn't put up a fight as Corey led her upstairs to her room where she began to pace the floor.

Alyssa tried to calm herself down, but she couldn't. The argument that she had with her father burned her up inside and she couldn't shake it for nothing. The lack of support she got from her father shouldn't have surprised her, but she figured he wouldn't support her because of how dangerous her job was or something on the lines of that, but it was for a reason she didn't think of. She also wasn't surprised by Andrea's will to defend their father, but instead of being the voice of reason, she just took his side and didn't try to defend her at all. What kind of lawyer was she? Alyssa knew it was only a matter of time before their relationship went back to the way it was. Andrea was always going to kiss their father's ass, but that was the final straw and Drea's uppity ass was going to pay. Alyssa began plotting her revenge in her head as she tuned Corey out.

***

Andrea couldn't believe how the past few days had gone. It was true that they had some good moments, but the shocking truths had definitely outweighed the good. When she reached out to her sisters to come home for Thanksgiving, she had no idea whatsoever that it would turn out in the manner that it did. They had their differences growing up, with her and Lexi being the closest and Alyssa and Anastasia having each other's backs, but she had no idea that the middle sisters took the sibling rivalry to heart as much as they did. If she didn't know before, the Thanksgiving holidays had proved it. It may seem crazy, but she was already plotting thinking ahead to Christmas in hopes that everyone would come back on a more positive note. Maybe their dad's sermon in a few hours would make everyone forget about all of the drama.

Even though Drea still felt some type of way about how her parents treated them, she would never disrespect them. She didn't even cuss her dad out for the stunt that he pulled the Sunday before, so she wasn't going to let Alyssa disrespect him either. Andrea could tell by the slick comment Lyssa made during their argument that she knew about her pregnancy, but she wasn't about to be punked or blackmailed. They all knew how their parents felt about them setting examples. The pregnancy shit had Andrea feeling like a failure and she hadn't even had time to figure out how to break the news to her parents.

"We whooped that nigga asssss last night didn't we… couldn't even tell you was pregnant and shit the way you was throwing them blows," Lexi squealed.

"He deserved it… how you gon screw your wife's best friend," Drea shook her head.

"I can't wait to get that hoe... bitch better be glad she ran!"

"You know... we all have our disagreements, but we do know how to stick together when needed. I do hate all the tension between us, but I real life thought it was just a friendly sibling rivalry growing up," Drea expressed.

"It wassss... them two just special. Don't let them get to you sis," Lexi waved her off.

"You think everybody will come back for Christmas?"

"Helllll naw!!!!! You can forget that shit, Drea... I'm surprised the other two still even here!"

"Well Ima try... we getting older, mommy and daddy getting older, and we need to do better!"

"I come and visit anyway, but I'm just saying... it's gon take some good ass convincing to get the New York hoes to come!"

"Lexi be nice... it's Sunday."

"Sis, I'm just ready for Monday, so I can get outta here... all this shit has been a lot. I gotta get back to the A and find me somewhere else to stay. Bre bitch ass," Lexi mumbled.

"We all need to go out tonight... we all got shit going on, but we gotta be there for each other."

"Yeah yeah yeah... let's just finish getting ready for church. I prolly need to smoke me a blunt before we go just in case."

Andrea ignored that comment from her baby sister and finished getting ready for church. She couldn't lie and say that there weren't a million and one thoughts running through her mind, but she had to be the big sister and push through. Ever since they were kids, it was true that Drea took on the motherly role and tried to keep everyone together. Somewhere along the line, the middle two had started to resent her for it and it made her start wonder if she was really fit to be anyone's mom. After looking at herself in the mirror one last time, Andrea admired herself in her black dress she had picked up from Ross. She slipped on some Steve Madden wedges and sprayed some light blue perfume on and was good to go. Andrea walked to the kitchen and grabbed a banana and a bottle of water, then yelled for Lexi to hurry up.

They didn't even try to go to Sunday school, but at eleven o'clock sharp, Andrea pulled into the parking lot of New Jerusalem Baptist Church. Lexi was on her phone pretty much the entire trip. Drea knew that her sister was still feeling some type of way about her parents knowing the lifestyle that she was living, but she decided that she would talk to her at a later date about it.

"Come on, let's go," Drea prompted her baby sister, so that they could go on inside.

They walked inside and the usher greeted them with a smile and hugged them both. Andrea led the way up the aisle to take a seat near their mom where Anastasia and Alyssa already were. Devotion was starting and their father hadn't come from his study yet, which was good for them because they knew that he would have something slick to say since they weren't already in their seats. Even Andrea didn't get a pass on being late for church and she was the favorite. Andrea was very surprised to see Aunt Shirley at church. Lexi squeezed in and sat down beside her, so Drea took the seat on the end.

Andrea didn't miss the eye roll that Alyssa gave her when she sat down. She said a silent prayer that they would have a peaceful day and hopefully end the weekend on good terms. Abraham made his way to the pulpit right after the offering was taken up, wearing his black robe with red crosses on each side. He smiled at his congregation and took a stand behind the podium. Andrea recited his favorite scripture along with him, and when he was done, she knew that he was about to call the choir around to sing, but she was surprised when he took a different route.

"As you all can see, I have my entire family here with me today." He motioned towards everyone, then continued after there was a round of applause including some "Hallelujah's, Amen's, and God is good" cheers.

"My oldest daughter, Andrea who y'all see all the time, took it upon herself to gather up her sisters and get them home for the holidays. It has been an interesting few days, and I'm gonna have to pray for all of my children!"

"We gotta keep our children covered in prayer all the time, pastor!"

"That's right, Sis Buford!" he acknowledged.

"Oh shit… what is Abraham ass bout to do?" Aunt Shirley mumbled, but Drea heard her loud and clear and silently wondered the same thing.

"I want all of my daughters to come up here. I gotta do what the Lord has laid on my heart… Andrea has it altogether, but she's about to get married and we all can stand some prayer, right?"

"That's right pastor!" several saints said in unison.

"Y'all go on babies... he just wants to pray," their mom whispered to them.

"His ass needs prayer," Aunt Shirley said after she bent down and took a sip from her flask.

Since Andrea was on the end, she got up first, but she couldn't help but to notice that her sisters shared the same scowl that was on her face. She had talked to her daddy and told him that Joseph just wasn't the one for her, and he acted like he understood, but clearly, he hadn't. Flashbacks of the Sunday before ran through Andrea's mind as she slowly made her way towards the alter. She felt the stares of saints on her and her sisters and had begun to tune out whatever her dad was saying until she heard him say Joseph's name.

"Drea you stand to the left, and Lyssa, Lexi, and Stasia y'all stand to the right," Abraham said, then motioned for Joseph to stand next to Andrea. She took a deep breath because she felt herself getting ready to explode at any given moment.

"Why don't you tell him the real deal instead of going along with this foolishness?" Drea harshly whispered to Joseph.

Instead of him responding, she watched as his eyes locked with the choir director's and she shook her head. Andrea listened as her father went on and on and on about how she was about to make him proud by marrying the son of Deacon Jones, who was also his best friend.

"Daddy, I'm not marrying Joseph... he's in love with Julius!" Andrea blurted out before she could stop herself, while pointing at the choir director.

A series of gasps and ooh's and ahh's could be heard throughout the sanctuary. Joseph took off running out of the sanctuary while his dad stood there in shock along with Abraham.

"Drea... how could you? I would expect this from... why? How could..."

"From who dad? Me or Anastasia, huh... because we all know that Drea is your favorite and you got her sitting up on a pedestal while you look down on the rest of us!" Alyssa fumed.

"Alysa Holiday, you know that's not true... if you would have given me time I was going to..."

"I don't care to hear it... it's been this way for years," Alyssa kept talking while Anastasia tugged on her and tried to get her quiet, all to no avail. "Just so you know... your precious daughter that you praised for not getting pregnant out of wedlock is pregnant!!!" Alyssa continued and Anastasia finally put her hand over her mouth.

"You little..." Drea stormed towards Alyssa, but Lexi stepped in her path.

"Come on, Drea; let's go outside," Lexi whispered.

"Andrea... is this tr..." Abraham could be heard over the microphone saying, but before he finished the word, a loud thump was heard and he fell to the floor.

"Oh my God!" different people yelled.

"Daddy!" the girls took off running towards the pulpit.

"He's not breathing… call 911," was the last thing Andrea heard Deacon Jones yell before everything around her turned black.

Chapter 1

Andrea's eyes fluttered as she adjusted to the light in the room. As she laid there, she began to process everything that had happened. The past few days had been a nightmare, and Drea started regretting the fact that she had mad everyone come home. She hated to feel that way because she really wanted to have a closer bond with all of her sisters, but the feelings didn't appear to be mutual.

"Oh my God... daddy! I gotta find my daddy!" Drea panicked when her mind went back to church and seeing her dad fall to the floor in the pulpit, and then a nurse ran into the room.

"Calm down, Ms. Holiday. You don't want to cause any extra stress on your body; it might affect the baby," the nurse sweetly explained.

It was then that reality smacked Andrea in the face. Even after taking all of the home pregnancy tests, she still had a few doubts. To hear the words come from the nurse confirmed everything. She was really going to be someone's mom.

"I was given instructions to tell you that your dad is just fine. He did have a mild heart attack, but he is fine and only being kept for observations."

"I have to see him... where is he? What time is it?" Drea stood up.

"It's a little after midnight. I'm sure your dad is resting. Your sister left a little while ago and said to tell you that she would call you tomorrow."

"Lexi?"

"Yeah, that was her name."

Andrea listened as the nurse tried to keep her calm. She was at River Oaks hospital and was informed that her dad was at Baptist. When the nurse told Andrea that she was fine and they were only keeping her for observation, she decided that she wasn't about to stay any longer. She knew that her parents were probably disappointed in her, but she had to get to them. Her body must have been tired for her to sleep for so long, but she was alert and ready to make a move at the moment. All kinds of thoughts were running through Andrea's head as she hurried to get dressed in her clothes that were right beside her in a bag on the counter.

"You're actually fine to go, but you'll need to schedule an appointment with your OBGYN soon," the nurse informed her.

She thanked her, then grabbed her purse and headed out. Andrea grabbed her phone from her purse and then clicked the Uber app. She hoped that there was one nearby, or she would have to take a cab. Luck must have been on her side, because there was one only five minutes away. She requested it and made her way towards the exit. She wasn't even in a regular room, she was still in one of the emergency examination rooms. Once the Uber driver called back and informed her that he was pulling up, Drea made her way outside. Once she was in, she called Lexi, then, Anastasia and Alyssa. All of their phones went straight to voicemail and it annoyed Andrea.

Since there wasn't much traffic out, the driver arrived at Baptist about ten minutes later. Andrea thanked him and got out. She went to the receptionist desk and gave them her father's name. When she found out that he was on the third floor, she went to the elevator and headed up.

Andrea took a deep breath, then said a silent prayer when she reached room 3158. She slowly pushed the door open and eased inside. Her mom was sitting in a chair on the right side of the bed holding Abraham's hand; she looked up as soon as Drea made it inside. Andrea's eyes went straight to her dad's and he was lying there looking so peaceful and she prayed that was the case.

"How is he?" Drea finally found her voice when she made it to the bed.

"He's gonna be fine… but, you girls really did do a number on him… especially you," Victoria sadly confessed.

Andrea sighed because she knew that her mom was right. Out of all of the girls, she was supposed to be the one that they looked up to, but there she was in a situation that she knew her parents had preached and preached about all of their lives.

"How long will he have to stay in here?" Drea finally broke the silence and inquired.

"Probably just a few days."

"Where's Lexi them at? Downstairs somewhere?"

"They all had early flights."

"So, they left while daddy is here in the hospital?" Drea fumed.

"He's gonna be okay."

Andrea heard her mom talking, but she wasn't really listening to her. She knew that everyone had lives, and so did she, but she would do whatever it took to make sure that her parents were okay. That was always the difference between her and them. She didn't expect much from Lexi since she was the baby, but she knew that Anastasia and Alyssa knew better. Instead of speaking on her feelings at the moment, she rubbed her dad's hand as he slept and said another prayer. She pulled a chair up, then sat down because she didn't plan on leaving until she heard the words from the doctor, that her dad was going to be okay, with her own ears.

The next morning, Andrea finally left the hospital a little after nine when the doctor left her dad's room. She hadn't slept worth shit in that uncomfortable ass chair, but she toughed it out. Her mom didn't speak on any of the drama, but Drea knew it was only because she was worried about her husband. He was going to be in the hospital at least until the next day as long as all of the tests came back fine. When Hannah pulled up, she hopped straight in with her friend and instructed her to take her home, then filled her in on all of the drama that had transpired.

"Oh... my... gawwddd!! Are you fuckin serious? Y'all need a damn Holiday reality show," Hannah laughed after Drea was finally done.

"This shit ain't funny, Hannah!" Drea rolled her eyes.

"Oh bitch, but it is. Now, if this was anybody else we would be rolling. Lexi stripping and sexing her best friend, y'all done beat the hell out of Anastasia's husband at a hotel, Alyssa's secretive ass done finally came clean annndddd she stepped up to Mr. Holiday, then put you on blast at church. I'm sorry bout your dad... he gon be alright, but this shit is a whole damn book. Nah fuck that, it's a movie!" Hannah emphasized.

"Damn, I hate I didn't come to church." She continued.

"It is a lot... it would be funnier if it was someone else though. But, can you believe all them hoes left while daddy was laying there in the hospital?"

"Uhhh yeah. None of em even wanted to come. It is wrong, but you asked if I could believe it and I can... but, your dad will be alright."

"I'm still gon cuss their asses out for being so inconsiderate."

"Wouldn't be Andrea Holiday if you didn't," Hannah chuckled.

Hannah pulled up to Andrea's house and she noticed that her car was there. She had no idea who had brought it from the church, but she was thankful. Andrea thanked her friend for picking her up and told her that she would get up with her later. She had a big case in a few days that she needed to execute. Pretty much everything was done and in place, but Andrea's routine was to double and triple check everything. The first thing she did was call Lexi when she walked in. The phone rang about two times, then connected. Andrea was expecting to hear Lexi answer by fussing and saying she was sorry for leaving, but that wasn't the case at all.

Chapter 2

After an hour and a half flight, a three-hour layover in Charlotte, and a quick nap on her second flight, Lexi couldn't contain her excitement when the pilot announced that they were landing into Hartsfield Jackson Atlanta International Airport. She still couldn't believe all of the shit that had gone down the past few days. While descending, Lexi thought back to the conversation that she had with her mom on Thanksgiving night when she pulled her to the side.

"Alexis, I'm very disappointed in you. You know that you don't have to degrade yourself in such a manner... did we do something wrong as parents?"

Lexi heard her mom loud and clear, and she knew that sooner or later she was going to be questioned. Even though she was grown, she felt like a little kid who had just gotten caught eating a snack after she was told to go to bed. She was tired of the pressure of always having to do the right thing, which was why she was planning on staying in Atlanta after graduation. Lexi told herself that it was time to stand up for herself and be the adult that she was.

"No mommy... y'all did everything right. Maybe it was too right. My decisions don't have anything to do with how y'all raised me. What I do, it's for me and I don't feel like I'm degrading myself."

"And Bre... lord Jesus. You've created a mess for yourself, Lexi."

"Mommy I'm..."

"A big mess. Lexi, we didn't send you over there to Atlanta to get into this kinda foolishness," Abraham walked in and chimed in on the conversation.

55

"Dad, I'm not being mean, but y'all didn't really send me anywhere. I had to beg to go and y'all finally just gave in."

"Don't get smart with your dad, Alexis Holiday!" her mom scolded.

"I'm not getting smart, mommy. I'm just saying."

She listened to her parents as they talked about how she was a child a God and she had to make better choices and blah blah blah. It was really her dad, but she knew that her mom was going to agree with whatever he said no matter what. Lexi was just ready for them to finish talking so that she could lie and agree, then get out of there. J.R. was on her mind and she wanted to call just to hear his voice.

"Do you understand, Alexis?"

"Yes sir. I understand," Lex replied and walked out with her mind on how much money she was going to make the next weekend.

"Welcome to Atlanta where the current temperature is 56 degrees," the flight attendant interrupted Lexi from her thoughts.

After Lexi got off the plane and made her way towards baggage claim, she finally powered her phone back on. She had turned it off right after she talked to J.R. the night before and asked him to pick her up from the airport. When he agreed, she didn't want to be bothered with anyone else. Lexi already knew that Drea was going to call and cuss her out for leaving without saying anything, but she was prepared to hear her mouth. They fussed, but they always made up. Lexi scrolled through the 426 unread text messages that she had to see if any were worth clicking on and replying to, and the only one that was worth her time was from Marcus, so she texted him and told him that she would call him later.

Lexi called J.R. after she got her luggage and he told her that he was already outside. As she made her way through the big ass airport, she clicked on her emails and almost shouted for joy when both of her classes of the day had been cancelled. In the beginning, Lexi hated that she had one professor for two classes, but it really worked out in her favor. She spotted J.R.'s ride and headed that way. He got out and grabbed her luggage, then she hopped in.

"I need a blunt," was the first thing she said when he got back in.

"Lil mama done had a few rough days," he teased as he grabbed a blunt out of the ash tray and handed it to her.

Lexi wasted no time firing it up and taking a couple of pulls. The weed instantly mellowed her out and she closed her eyes and relaxed for a moment.

"What time you got class?"

"I don't today and I'm happy as hell about it," Lexi replied and the thought of chilling at home alone with J.R. caused her to smile because she knew that Bre would be gone all day.

"Wanna get something to eat?" J. R. asked as she passed the blunt to him.

"Yup… I'm hungry as shit."

"Bet!"

J. R. received a phone call and Lexi could tell that it was business, so she clicked on the Facebook app and scrolled through. She hadn't really been on much in the past few days considering the drama that her family had been going through, and the first thing she saw was a struggling Thanksgiving plate. She didn't know why Facebook thought she wanted to pick up where she left off instead of seeing the current posts, but that nasty ass looking plate made her close the app completely and head over to Snap Chat to view some stories. At least she knew it would only be stuff from the last twenty-four hours.

J.R. ended his call and pulled up to a place called The Flying Biscuit Café on Piedmont Avenue a little after eight. Lexi had heard of the place, but she had never been there before. They made their way inside and were seated promptly. When the waitress arrived, they already had their orders in mind and placed them. As soon as she left, Lexi wasted no time sparking up a conversation.

"So, did you miss me?"

"Hell naw," he replied and then Lexi picked up her fork like she was about to throw it at him.

"I'm just playing, shordy... you know I missed yo lil feisty ass," he continued.

"I missed yo big head, too... these past few days been crazy as fuck yo!"

"What happened? Did the pastor find out his baby girl was the top dancer at Blue Flame?" J.R. laughed.

When he saw that Lexi wasn't cracking a smile, he stopped abruptly.

"Tell me that shit didn't happen. I was just playing."

"That's exactly what happened, but I don't even wanna get into all that right now. They so hurt about that, but it was so many other secrets that came out and my daddy had a heart attack yesterday at church," Lexi explained.

"Got damn... is pops alright?"

"Yeah... mommy said he will be just fine. I wanted to stay, but I really needed to get away."

"Damn... if you ever need to get back over there in a hurry, just let me know and I got you."

"That's so sweet of you... thank you," Lexi smiled.

The waitress walked up and sat their food down in front of them. Lexi poured some hot syrup on her pancakes and dug in, while J.R. ate his steak and cheese omelet. They talked throughout breakfast and got to know each other more. It seemed as if they had known each other for years with how comfortable they were with each other. Lexi was still in awe that he still even piqued her interest because after talking to a dude a couple of times, she would normally put them on the blocked list. His style, intellect, and not to mention, his A1 sex game had her open.

"What you smiling about, shordy?"

"I was just thinking about last Wednesday night and how I want an encore."

"Oh yeah?" he smirked.

"Hell yeah... no one is at my place, so let's hurry up."

She must have said the magic words because J.R. was done eating in less than five minutes, and so was she. Lexi reached into her purse to grab her wallet when the waitress brought the check over, but J.R. stopped her.

"When you wit me, I got you… aight?" he told her.

"I can help out sometimes, nigga," Lexi playfully rolled her eyes.

Thirty minutes later, J.R. was pulling up at Lexi's place and her pussy began to tingle at just the thought of what was about to go down once they were alone. As soon as he parked, she grabbed her keys out of her purse and headed upstairs with J.R. right behind her. The apartment was quiet just as Lexi expected. J.R. asked to use the bathroom as soon as they walked in, so Lexi took her luggage from him and pointed to the door on the right to the half bath. She pulled her vibrating phone out of her pocket as she rolled her luggage toward her room and became puzzled when she heard the TV on because she knew for a fact that she didn't leave it on. The sight of Bre laying on her bed chilling like everything was all good sent Lexi into a rage.

"Hey boo," Bre smiled.

"You dirty bitch!" Lexi screamed as she lunged towards her.

Bre never had the chance because Lexi jumped on her and sent blows to every inch of her body. She talked shit while beating her ass like a parent did while whooping a child. Bre's cries and screams didn't faze Lexi not even the least little bit. She was going to beat her to a bloody pulp.

"Stooopppp…. I'm sorry! I didn't mean to…" Bre cried.

"Fuck that! You stupid bitch!" Lexi screamed and continued kicking Bre's ass.

"Yo, what the fuck goin on in here?" J.R. came rushing in and grabbed Lexi.

"Naw, fuck that… let me go!" she struggled to get away from J.R. all to no avail.

The sight of J.R. must have given Bre some courage because she jumped up and began screaming louder as she charged at Lexi. Before she made it, J.R. shifted his body and pushed Lexi behind him.

"CHILL THE FUCK OUT!!" he fumed as both of them stopped all movement.

"You know what? Fuck you, Lexi… clearly you done chose this nigga over me and I ain't bout to be disrespected. Fuck both of y'all!" Bre spat and limped out of Lexi's room.

Lexi paced the floor when J.R. finally put some space between them. Lexi looked down at the floor and saw Drea's name on her screen and the call had been going for almost three minutes. Instead of hanging up, she picked it up and told her sister that she would call her back. Andrea made her say that she was okay before she allowed her to hang up, and Lexi assured her that she was fine.

"You know you gon have to tell me what the fuck is up wit you, ol girl… this shit don't even make no sense."

Lexi sighed and after a few short moments, she prepared herself to be straight up with J.R. about her relationship with Bre.

"Gone ahead, shorty, I'm listening," J.R. said, taking a seat on the edge of Lexi's California King bed.

She stopped pacing the floor finally and looked over at him, placing both hands on her hips.

"Long story short, three years ago, our freshman year, we started fuckin around and we never stopped," she stated, shrugging her shoulders. "Things started getting messy when I let it be known that I wasn't on no relationship shit and that's when the bitch started bugging out," she continued.

J.R. shook his head before using his hand to smooth over his trimmed beard.

"At my parents' house over the break, the crazy bitch told everyone about us, not to mention, the fact that I stripped. I mean, the bitch really came, fucked shit up, and left," Lexi finished off, taking a seat next to an attentive J.R.

The expression on J.R.'s face let it be known that he was shocked beyond words. He just sat there and waited, wondering if she had some more to tell.

"And I'm sorry about not being upfront with you about all this in the beginning..." she started to say before he cut her off.

"Look man, that's yo business and I wouldn't expect a motherfucker just to bust out and say no shit like "aw yeah, me and my best friend fuckin" .... You know what I mean?"

Lexi felt a little relieved when she heard him say that. It kind of made her feel better coming clean. Although her secrets came out the wrong way, the fact that she didn't have to hide shit anymore made her heart and mind feel lighter.

"My life is all crazy," she said, placing her face inside the palm of her hands.

"Yeah baby, you are a little fucked up, but it'll be straight," J.R. promised her as he rubbed her back.

The slightest touch from him turned her on, even though, she just dealt with some crazy shit, she got the urged to suck his dick. Lexi raised her head and looked over at her opened door, before she slowly rose to her feet, attempting to close the door, but J.R. pulled her back down, onto his lap.

"You know you gotta deal with shorty and that situation. You can't keep putting it off," he said, with both arms wrapped around her tight.

"I know, I'm going to look for a place first thing in the morning, she can have this shit," Lexi replied, as she pulled away from his embrace and proceeded to close and lock her door.

Once Lexi reached the door, she noticed Bre walking down the hallway towards her bedroom, Lexi rolled her eyes and slammed the door before turning back towards J.R.

"I've had a long week; can I just get some dick and forget about it all?" Lexi flirted, licking her lips and pulling her shirt over her head.

She seductively walked over to where J.R. was sitting. A smile crept across his face while he patiently waited to see what was next, but before she could reach him, a screaming Bre busted into the room. Lexi quickly turned around just in time to catch her running towards her with a butcher knife in hand. Lexi froze up, it hadn't quite dawned on her what was happening. If it wasn't for J.R. and his quick actions, Bre would have stabbed the shit out of Lexi.

"Bitch, is you stupid?" J.R. screamed, as he pushed Bre to the ground.

"No bitch, but I bet you take yo ass to jail for touching me," Bre cried out as she rubbed the back of her head.

"Jail??" J.R... laughed.

"Call them muthafuckers then!" J.R. said before pulling out a pistol and aiming it at Bre's head.

"It's one thing to play with my shorty, but a nigga don't play those police games, ma," he continued.

Lexi smiled at the sight of J.R. defending her, but she smiled even bigger as she looked down at a terrified Bre.

Lexi still couldn't believe that shit had gotten as out of hand as it did; however, she took that opportunity to make herself feel a little better. Lexi lifted up her foot and kicked Bre in the face with her size seven Timberland boot. Bre yelled out in pain as she covered her now leaking mouth.

"I should let her kick yo ass," J.R. threatened before grabbing Lexi by the arm and stepping over a crying Bre.

"Imma send somebody over here to pack up her shit and if you touch her shit while she's gone, I swear to God Imma kill you, bitch," J.R. spoke furiously.

Lexi watched his jaw tighten up and the spit fly from his mouth. It was then that she knew he meant business.

"Let's go!" he ordered.

Lexi followed his lead, but not before gulping up spit and slinging it out at Bre, who looked scared out of her mind.

"Bitch, don't think this is over!" Bre cried out, but her threats fell on deaf ears as Lexi walked out of the apartment she once shared with her best friend.

Chapter 3

Alyssa could've gotten down on her hands and knees and kissed her hardwood floors when she entered her condo that day. She walked into her bedroom and collapsed on her bed. It felt good to be back in the peace and tranquility of her own home and away from all of the family drama. She thought back to the previous day and tried to convince herself that what happened to her father wasn't her fault, but there was a twinge of guilt telling her that it was. After they got the word that their father was okay, Alyssa debated on whether she should stay. She didn't have to return to work for a few more days, but she would be damned if she stayed around her parents and older sister another minute.

Corey entered the room with her luggage in his hand and sat it next to the bed. He sat on the edge, grabbed her hand, and pulled her up so she was sitting next to him. In need of a serious sex session, Alyssa kissed his lips passionately and her hand was starting to make its way to the button of his jeans, until he stopped her. She tried to fight her way around him, but to no avail. With a look of confusion plastered on her face, Alyssa waited for him to explain.

"Look, I didn't say nothin' the entire flight home, but I gotta get this off my chest. That lil' stunt you pulled at the church was far from cool. Ya pops is laid up in the hospital and you act like you don't even care."

"Corey, I'm trying to fuck, wash up, and take a nap. I don't feel like talking about this right now." Alyssa got up from the bed, walking into the bathroom.

"You really had to get ya sister back like that? You couldn't be the bigger person and let that shit slide?" He followed her.

"No, I couldn't because when I needed Andrea to take my side against dad, she defended his ass. I wanted her to know how it feels to be viewed as a disappointment by our parents. I didn't think the news would cause my father to have a heart attack."

"So, how are you gonna handle this situation, Lyssa?"

"I'm not. Okay. I'm just going to let things be. Besides, now that I'm an FBI agent, I'm on my parent's shit list."

"And you're cool with that?"

"Why shouldn't I be? Shit has been this way for years now and to be honest, I don't think it's going to change," she admitted.

"Now, are you going to give me some dick or what?"

Corey walked over to her and tossed her over his shoulder like she was paper weight and carried her back into the bedroom. He placed her on the bed and stripped her naked. Pulling her to the edge of the bed, he dropped to his knees, placed her legs on his shoulders and dove in. Corey made love to her clit for over an hour causing her to cum a total of four times. As he began to undress himself, the ringing of his phone caused him to quickly put his clothes back on.

"Umm, where are you going?" Alyssa leaned up on her elbows.

"I gotta go, bae. Somethin' just came up. I'll call you lata."

Before she could respond, Corey dashed out the bedroom and the sound of the front door slamming shut, confirmed he was gone. Alyssa stayed stuck in the position he left her in for a few minutes before she got up and walked into the bathroom, running the water for her shower. She washed her body and hair before wrapping a towel around her and her wet hair. After blow drying her hair, Alyssa got dressed in a tank top, yoga pants, and ankle socks. She grabbed her backpack, pulled out her cell phone, and turned it on. Alyssa didn't expect to have so many text messages, phone calls and voicemails, but she figured they were from her family and decided not to check them. Grabbing her suitcase, she began to unpack.

The way Corey darted out her condo had her mind racing. Since they'd been dating, Corey was never in a hurry to leave her side the way he did that day and the fact that he left her in the middle of one of their love making sessions had her thinking the worst, but being as though that it was his first time doing something like that, she figured she would let it go. When she was finished putting away her clothes, her phone began to ring and she was happy to see that it was Kelly calling.

"Hey Boo. What's going on with you?" she answered.

"Hey girl. You don't know how much I missed you. My holiday was cool, but it wasn't the same without you. How was yours?"

"Giirrll, don't even get me started on my holiday. That shit was a mess from the time I got there until I left a few hours ago. The only fun I had was when we went to the club and when we whooped Stasia's husband's ass for cheating with her best friend," she stated dryly.

"Biittchh! You better give me the details and stop playing with my emotions!"

Alyssa gave Kelly the rundown of her family gathering and she didn't miss a beat. She didn't forget to mention the argument she had with father and sister or how her act of vengeance put her father in the hospital. The silence on the other end of the phone let her know that her friend didn't agree with what she did.

"Aight, Kels, speak your mind."

"You know you're my best friend, so I'm not going to tell you nothing wrong. So, here it is. You were dead wrong for what you did in that church. It's one thing to be upset with your folks, but to air y'all dirty laundry out like that is unacceptable. Especially, in the house of the Lord. I'm surprised your ass ain't get struck by lightning or some shit."

"Oh goodness. You sound like Corey." She rolled her eyes.

"Look, I know you and your sisters don't get along and I don't agree with how your father demanded you to leave your job because of a past incident, but all you have is your family and you have to fix that."

Alyssa listened to Kelly ramble on about how family was important and how Andrea needed her more than ever because she was pregnant. She ended up cutting the conversation short, but promised to link up with her sometime throughout the week. Alyssa didn't want to admit that her bestie was right. A part of her wanted to continue to hold a grudge and be mad, but she couldn't. She knew that Andrea was catching hell from her parents because of the fact that she was pregnant without a husband and Alyssa knew first-hand what she was going through being as though she was also a disappointment to their father. She made a mental note to reach out to Andrea, but it would be in her own time and no one else's.

Chapter 4

Anastasia lay sprawled across her bed with her sun blocking curtains drawn, and her mind on the events of the past week. She had yet to speak to Richard's dog ass, but that wasn't from lack of trying... on his part anyway. Since her and her sisters had beat his ass in the hotel he'd called her over one hundred times, but she'd ignored them all. She'd considered blocking him, but knew there was no way for her to shut him completely out due to Kyler. At least he had the common sense not to show his ass up to their house. She couldn't help, but chuckle at the fact that he was probably scared to show his face after the way they'd jumped his ass. He had to have been shocked that they had all come together just to fight him, knowing that they didn't get along normally. But, one thing Anastasia knew was that no matter their differences, her and her sisters would always have each other's backs against an outsider. She just wished that Lizz's hoe ass had been there to catch some of that fade. The only thing that made her feel any better about the situation was knowing that New York was only so big, and she knew that sooner or later she would see her.

The buzzing of her phone brought her out of her thoughts and she glanced at the screen to see that Alyssa was calling once again. Normally, she would have answered for her favorite sister, but she was just too into her own feelings to deal with anything else at the moment. Either she was calling just to talk and see where her head was at or she wanted to discuss their father. Neither of those topics was on Anastasia's list of things to do at the moment, so she let her phone ring until it went to voicemail. Unfortunately for her, no sooner than it stopped, it was right back going off. Pissed, she snatched it up and answered without looking to see who was calling.

"Stop fuckin' callin me!"

"Ummm…. Anastasia?" the timid voice of her new employee, Juanita, came through the line and she immediately felt like shit for yelling. She'd forgotten that fast that she had asked her to open up the shop today.

"I'm so sorry, hun; people have been blowing my phone up all day," she sighed.

She'd just hired Juanita to work the store for her right before she went home for the holidays. As soon as she had come into the store, Anastasia knew she would hire her. Besides, the fact that she was dressed to the nines and looked nowhere near her age of 46, her availability was pretty much open. Ms. Juanita was a newly widowed mother of two teenage boys and needed something to do with her spare time, which was more often than she cared for. Her and Anastasia clicked right away, so she hired her on the spot.

"Oh, well I'm here at the shop and um…. my key won't unlock the doors," she said with confusion laced all through her voice.

"Oh," Anastasia frowned. "Did you use the gold key?" she asked, not too concerned at the moment because she knew that there were at least five different keys on the key ring she had given to her. There was one for the front door, one for the back, the register key, the safe key, and also the key to her office.

"Yes, I have each key designed so that I don't forget what it goes too, but these locks seem like they've been changed."

Anastasia's eyes bucked at what she'd said, because the only way that would be possible was for Richard to have taken his lame ass down there and changed her locks.

Before she knew it, she was down the stairs and slipping on her black Nike boots and coat.

"I'll be right there Juanita," she said reassuringly as she locked up the house and made her way over to her car.

Hanging up the phone, she called Richard's ass fuming. How dare he try to lock her out of something that belonged to her? It was just like him to try and force her hand, so that he could get a reaction. Of course, her calls went unanswered and she was forced to leave him a message.

"Richard, you got some fuckin' nerve changing the locks to my place of business, nigga! That ass whoopin' we gave you must not have been enough, because you just keep on tryin' me! You better answer this phone or bring yo old limp dick ass up here and give me a key or all hell is gon' break loose!"

What should have been at least a twenty-minute drive was split in half as she damn near burned rubber to get to her store. When she pulled up, Juanita was still standing out front and her eyes almost popped out of her head at how Anastasia pulled up. She barely put the car in park before she hopped out and stomped over to the door, simultaneously fumbling with her keys until she got to the one she was looking for. She could hear Juanita saying something to her, but the loud pulsing in her ears made it impossible to understand. As she tried to force the key into the lock she called Richard again, instantly getting even more pissed when he sent her to voicemail.

"Uhhhh... this nigga!" she growled, hanging up and kicking at the door, when an idea came to her. She turned her attention to a stunned Juanita.

"Do you need a ride?"

"Uh sure, you know I rode the bus over," she stammered with a raised brow.

"Well, I'll take you home," Anastasia told her with a firm nod, before heading back to her car without waiting for a reply.

She was sitting inside with the car running and in gear by the time Juanita made it over to her and as soon as she had her door closed, Anastasia pulled off into traffic.

"Maybe you should slow down," she suggested, after she had clicked in her seatbelt.

"I got something that I need to take care of Juanita. I'll make sure that you get home safely, I promise," Anastasia reassured her and continued to speed down the street.

The whole time she dialed Richard back to back never getting an answer. By the time she stopped in front of Juanita's building, the lady was scrambling to get out of the car. Before she could close the door, Anastasia made sure to let her know that everything would be straightened out by tomorrow. With an uneasy look, she gave Anastasia a nod, closed her car door, and hurried away.

She didn't have time to dwell on how crazy she may have looked to her, because she needed to be on her way to Richard's job to tear into his ass. The way Anastasia was burning through the New York streets, it was no wonder she didn't get into an accident or get pulled over. Somehow, she ended up parking crooked in a handicapped spot in the lot of Richard's job. She didn't even have time to thank God that she'd made it safe because she was too busy rushing out of the car and into the building.

"Good morning, Ana." the security guard, Russ, greeted her as she entered.

"Hey," Anastasia managed to get out as she damn near ran past him and to the elevators.

Once she heard the ding and the doors slid open on the ninth floor, she flew to Richard's closed office door and walked in without knocking. He sat behind his desk as if he was expecting her with a slick ass grin on his face and his arms behind his head.

"You, sorry son-of-a-bitch! How you gonna go and change the locks on my shit?" she fumed, walking up to his desk and slamming her purse down on it.

"Well, hello to you too dear," he said smartly, standing and making his way to the door.

He looked out to make sure that they didn't have anybody's attention before closing it softly and coming back to stand before her.

"Now, what's the problem?"

"Nigga, don't give me that shit! You know exactly what the fuck I'm talkin bout; you changed the locks on my store!" she shouted, clapping her hands between each word, while he grinned in her face.

"Well, technically it's mine; it is in my name." He shrugged casually further pissing her off. "Did you think that after we got a divorce, that you would leave with anything more than what you came with?"

"You're fuckin' crazy if you think I won't be leaving this shit with at least half of everything you own.... my shop included."

"Oh, really? And why is that?" he teased chuckling.

"Cause you was fuckin' my whole friend for I don't know how long, why the fuck else?" She didn't know where Richard had all of a sudden gotten his balls from, but she was ready to snatch them bitches off and put them back in her purse.

"Ana, didn't I tell you that I already have proof of your affair and I'm sure that you were messing around with that thug long before I started fuckin Lizz."

"I..." she started, but he cut her clean off.

"Let's be clear, Anastasia. If you go through with this divorce, not only will you leave with the same thing you came with, I'll make sure to paint you out as an unfit parent," he said, bringing his face close to hers.

"You already don't have a steady source of income without me, and not to, that nigga you call yourself messing with ain't shit, but a bum ass thug."

"If you think that you're taking my son or my store, you got another got damn thing comin!" she shouted, raising her arm to slap him.

He stopped her by grabbing ahold of her wrist and pulling her towards him. Anastasia's mouth dropped open as she took in his face. He wasn't the Richard that she knew. He looked down at her with his eyes narrowed angrily and his lips drawn into a tight line. It looked like the few bruises that her and her sisters had given him weren't nearly as bad as she thought that they were, and she found herself wishing that they could have done more damage.

"Oh, I can and I will! You know it's possible, Anastasia. You wouldn't have a leg to stand on in court." Anastasia could feel her anger radiating through her, but she didn't know what to do with herself. A part of her wanted to fight his ass and another part wanted to take heed to what he was saying to her.

"Fuck you, Richard!"

"Fuck me?" he laughed bitterly.

"Yeah, fuck you!"

"You always had a foul ass mouth, Ana," he grunted, causing her to look upside his head at how he talked shit about her mouth and cussed at the same time.

"Listen, I want you to drop this whole divorce thing, and let that fuckin' hoodlum know it's over or else you gone lose everything that you think you got … including Kyler." He pushed her away from him, then went back to sit behind his desk as if nothing even happened. "I'll give you a few days to consider, you can see yourself out."

Stunned, Anastasia didn't know what to say. Richard had never spoken to her like that before and he most definitely had not ever threatened her. She stood in the middle of the office blinking as Richard sat and got back to work as if she had left already. Without saying anything, she turned on her heels and stumbled out of his office, even more fucked up and angry than she had been when she'd gotten there. Basically, Richard was saying that in order for her to have her son and business, she had to stay in an unhappy marriage with his ass and lose D'Mani, while he continued to fuck Lizz. She shook her head and made her way to the elevators with her eyes down in defeat and ended up running smack into someone.

"Oh, I'm sorry, Ana. How are you?" she looked up to see Harold's pasty-faced ass with a huge grin.

She shrugged out of his grip and power walked away from his ass before she could say something that would make him look at her husband and his wife in a different light. In a daze, she made it down to her car and drove the speed limit all the way home wondering if D'Mani and her freedom were worth the things that she was about to go through with Richard? She did know one thing though and that was that he wasn't taking her son or her business and she would bet her life on that.

Chapter 5

As promised, Abraham was released from the hospital the following day. Andrea sat at her desk in tears as she recalled the conversation that she had with her mom that morning. She thought that her mom was joking when she told her that Deacon Jones would be picking them up and they didn't need her to. Her mom tried to smooth it over by saying that she knew she had work to do, but Andrea couldn't believe it. She did in fact have a lot of work to complete, but her family always came first and there was nothing in the world that would change that. Andrea felt her iPhone vibrating on the desk. When she glanced over at it, she saw that it was Hannah calling, so she slid the bar across to answer and put the phone on speaker since her office door was closed.

"Hey Hannah… what you got going on?"

"Just calling to tell you to clear your schedule for two o'clock."

"Why?" Drea quizzed.

"Because I made you an appointment. I know your stubborn ass is gonna wait until the last minute to do it, so God mommy stepped up and made it happen."

"You're so full of shit. I don't wanna…"

"I don't wanna hear it. Finish up everything from your case, and then I'll meet you there. Bye," Hannah said and hung up before Andrea could say another word.

It was crazy that her friend knew her so well. She had no plans on making an appointment anytime soon. Deep down, Drea felt like if she ignored the situation, it would just go away. She pushed the thoughts that she was having to the back of her mind and got back to work. Her client was due to arrive within the next thirty minutes, and Andrea needed to have everything done. She busied herself with printing off documents, labeling papers, making sure she had receipts and evidence in place, and by the time she was done, her phone rang and it was the administrative assistant letting her know that her elven o'clock had arrived. A few minutes later, she walked in.

"Hey there, Tanisha. How are you doing?"

"I'm good... just ready to get all of this over with."

"I understand that. Two more days and we can get the ball rolling."

Andrea got down to business. Tanisha filed for divorce because she caught her husband with a man, but he was contesting the divorce and not willing to pay alimony or child support. She wasn't working and depended on him for everything, which was why she had stayed with him for as long as she did, but the marriage had taken a toll on her mentally, as well as physically.

"It looks like everything we have is solid. Is there anything else that I need to know? I don't like to be blindsided by anything."

She noticed the shift in her client's demeanor, and asked the question again and told her that it was imperative that she is honest with her.

"That's everything," she finally answered.

"Well alrighty then... I'll see you bright and early Thursday morning. You shouldn't have to take the stand, but go over the notes just in case," Andrea said and dismissed her.

She finished up with a few more minor tasks, and before she knew it, it was already forty minutes after twelve. Andrea gathered her purse, phone, and other items that she was taking home and headed out. Since her friend had made her an appointment, her plan was to go and eat lunch, head to the doctor, and then go on home. The beauty of being flexible was what she loved about her job the most.

"I'm gone for the day, Sylvia. Just call me if you need me," Andrea told her assistant on her way out of the door.

"Have a great evening, Ms. Holiday and okay."

"Thanks honey, you do the same."

Andrea made her way outside and the weather had dropped tremendously. She was naturally cold natured, so even though she was dressed in warm clothing, it was still cold to her. When she hit the alarm to her black Benz, she noticed that it was time for a detail, so she made a mental note to call the guy in the neighborhood so that he could hook her up soon. Before pulling off, Andrea placed an online order to McAlister's. Time was ticking on by. She was going to eat inside, but she wanted to make sure it was ready upon arrival.

Twenty minutes later, Drea pulled up and parked in the first empty spot that she saw. She made her way inside and went to the register where call in and to-go orders were paid for and picked up. A few minutes later, she was sitting down with her rotel and chicken salad sandwich with no tomatoes. As Drea ate, she scrolled through Facebook and wondered when they were going to get a 'shut the fuck up' and a 'stop lying' button because nine posts out of every ten that was what she was saying to herself. By the time she finished with her food, Hannah was calling. Andrea loved her best friend and knew that she would need her more than ever in the upcoming months, so she wasn't going to cuss her out for being a pest.

"I'm on way, Hannah," Drea said as soon as the call connected.

"Bring ya ass. I'll see you in a few," Hannah said and hung up.

Thirty minutes later, Andrea made it to 165 Wimbledon Court. Her OBGYN had been Dr. Livingston for as long as she could remember. She ran across a lot of women who said they wouldn't be comfortable having a man as one, but Drea was the opposite. She couldn't imagine having a woman examine her. A thought of her baby sister popped into her head and caused her to giggle. She would be sure to joke around with her later. Andrea still was in shock that everyone left so soon, but the more that she thought about it, she did understand why. It hadn't been the best Thanksgiving holiday, so their asses probably ran to the airport.

As soon as Andrea got out of her car, she spotted her friend walking towards her with a big ass Kool-Aid smile on her face. For the life of her, she couldn't understand why she was so damn happy about the situation knowing how her family was.

"Don't frown at me, bitch. I'm happy because you're having a baby that I can spoil the shit out of. It's 2017, the marriage before having a baby shit just doesn't happen all the time anymore. God understands, he made us all," Hannah shrugged as if she was reading Andrea's mind.

"Uggghhhh… just come on."

They made their way inside and Andrea signed in. Her and Hannah made small talk. It was mainly Hannah throwing out baby names and planning a baby shower. Talking must have made the time fly on by because before they knew it, Andrea's name was being called. She made her way back and her height, weight, and blood pressure was checked, and then she was instructed to give a urine sample, then take a seat until her name was called again. Once she was done, she made her way to the seat beside Hannah.

In less than ten minutes, they were being led to another room. Dr. Livingston's nurse handed her a piece of cloth that she considered to be a gown and had Andrea to undress. When she came back in a few minutes later, she asked a million and one health related questions, and then finally confirmed Andrea's pregnancy. According to her last cycle, she was almost seven weeks pregnant. Even though it was already real, reality really set in at that moment. Andrea was about to be somebody's mommy.

"Lie back and we'll get an ultrasound," the nurse instructed.

Andrea did as she was told and a few moments later, she heard her baby's heartbeat and tears formed into her eyes. She laid there processing everything and prayed that her parents would come around soon. It was confirmed and everything appeared to be going well until she heard the nurse gasp.

"Oh my!"

"What's wrong?" Andrea and Hannah panicked.

"Umm look at this," she instructed them.

Andrea sat up and when the nurse pointed to screen, tears began to roll freely down her cheeks.

Chapter 6

Lexi woke up the next morning with a migraine that seemed to worsen as her eyes adjusted to the bright sun that was shining through the windows. She slowly sat up in the bed and looked around the room, it wasn't until then that it dawned on her that she was still at J.R.'s house. Lexi recollected her thoughts and replayed the events that happened as soon as she got back to Atlanta yesterday. A part of her wished that it was all a dream, but when she pulled the white sheets back and discovered the black bruises on her legs, she knew that in fact it wasn't a nightmare. Lexi let out a long sigh and rubbed her hands across the bruise before getting out the bed slowly. Not only was her skin fucked up, she was sore as shit. If she remembered the events correctly, she thought that she got the best of Bre, which made her wonder why the fuck she was aching like she got her ass beat.

"What's up, lil ugly." Lexi heard J.R.'s voice say from behind her.

She quickly snapped her neck around and stuck up her middle finger.

"Most niggaz say, what up beautiful," she corrected him as she stood to her feet and stretched.

"Niggaz who trying to fuck say that shit, I already hit so I'm good," J.R. laughed from the doorway.

Lexi picked up one of the few pillows that sat on the bed and threw it at him; it landed on the floor near his foot. J.R. picked the pillow up and tossed it back on the bed before walking in her direction.

"Aye, Imma put yo ass out my crib, keep throwing my shit," he replied, bending down slightly, placing a light kiss on her lips.

"I've been put out of better places," she giggled before heading towards the connecting bathroom.

Once inside the bathroom Lexi looked around, realizing she didn't have any of her belongings, but she seriously needed to brush her teeth at least.

"Baaeeeeee!" she yelled from the bathroom.

Moments later, J.R. appeared in the doorway.

"Please tell me you at least have a spare toothbrush and some type of soap that's not going to make my coochie itch."

J.R. laughed a little before turning around walking off.

"Yo punk ass ain't gon answer my question?" Lexi hissed, following behind him while he headed out the room and down the stairs.

J.R. led Lexi to the living room where there were bags full of clothes and shoes from Nordstrom's, Foot Locker, H&M, and Neiman Marcus laying around. Her faced screwed up with confusion as she looked at all the shit in front of her.

"My homies went and grabbed your shit from your crib. I also had one of my lil buddies do a little shopping for you. It's a Walmart bag over there somewhere with all that feminine shit you need. I'm about to go in the basement and handle some business. After you get out the shower, we can grab something to eat and chill," he stated, walking off leaving Lexi standing there in awe.

She took a few minutes and looked through all the things he picked up for her and she was pleasantly surprised. Whoever his "lil buddie" was had good taste, but what shocked her most was the fact that he kept his word and got all her clothes and things from the place she once shared with Bre. Lexi allowed her growling stomach to lead her back upstairs into the bathroom where she showered and got dressed. She was starving and ready to take J.R. up on his offer for food. She threw on a purple Nike jogging suit with the pair of Air Max 95s he got her and grabbed her phone before heading downstairs. On her way down, she noticed that she had a missed call from her mother and Drea. She decided to call her mother back first and Drea once she got into the car.

"Hey mommy. How's daddy doing?" was the first thing Lexi asked as soon as Victoria answered the phone.

"He's doing better, baby. He comes home tomorrow," her mother confirmed.

"Good! He really gave us a scare mommy," Lexi said in a saddened tone.

"Yea Alexis, he scared us all. You know you and your sisters really took a toll on him, with all y'all secrets and whatnot," she replied.

Lexi rolled her eyes, although she knew what her mother was saying was true, she just hated being the one to blame.

"I know and I'm going to call him as soon as I get off the phone with you to apologize."

"Well, he's resting right now. You can go ahead and call him later, baby," Victoria instructed.

Lexi and her mom talked about a few other things before the sound of their doorbell rang.

"Are you expecting company?" Lexi asked.

"Nope! I'm not sure who that is, but I'm going to call you back," Mrs. Holiday stated before ending the call.

Lexi got up from the couch she briefly rested on and headed downstairs to the basement to let J.R. know that she was ready to go. When she made it to the bottom of the stairs, she became speechless at the sight before her. J.R. was standing in front of his pool table, which had a pile of money on top of it. When she got a little closer, she noticed that there was nothing but one-hundred dollar bills scattered across it. With Lexi being a stripper, she was used to seeing large amounts of cash, however she had never witnessed shit like what she was staring at that very moment.

"You ready?" he asked, briefly looking up at her, then back down at the cash.

"Ummmm yeah, I guess," Lexi replied hesitantly.

"Aight, help me put this shit in my safe and then we can bounce."

Lexi helped J.R. carry the money to a safe that was located behind his 72-inch TV. They moved the funds in silence. Once they were done, they headed upstairs and out the door to grab something to eat. J.R. played an old Jeezy album as he cruised down 285 to Pappadeaux on Windy Hill Drive in Marietta.

"I got one baby momma

No bitch

No wife

Like Pac…. Ya need a thug in your life

A young to straight come through and beat it up

Let ya man be the freak

He can eat it up."

Both J.R. and Lexi rapped along to *Tear it up* a track on his first album featuring Lloyd. J.R. looked over at Lexi and smiled as if he was rapping the words to her. They listened to a few more tracks before he pulled into the parking lot of Lexi's favorite seafood place. Once he found a park, he killed the engine and hopped out while Lexi did the same.

"I'm surprised this motherfucker ain't crowded," J.R. said, opening the door for Lexi to walk through.

"Yeah me too," she replied, while they waited for the hostess to take them to their seats.

Within a matter of ten minutes, they were seated and a friendly waitress greeted them, ready to take their orders. Lexi ordered her regular, the Cajun Combo with a large Swamp Thang, while J.R. settled on Giant Shrimps and Grits and a Sprite. They made small talk while they waited on their food; however, Lexi wanted to ask questions about all that money he was counting. She knew that J.R. had to be a special type of drug dealer to be bringing in coins like that.

"So, what you got planned today?" he asked, taking a sip of soda.

"Well, I plan on applying for Grad-School and getting that shit out the way. I have class tonight at seven and then I'm headed to work after that," Lexi filled him in.

"Word? Grad-School? That's the shit I like to hear, but ummmm shordy, we need to talk about your job," J.R. replied.

"What about my job?" Lexi asked, finding herself instantly getting offended.

"Chill out, we will talk about it when we leave out of here, here come shordy with our food," J.R. let her know.

Lexi didn't utter another word, instead she dug right in and began eating as soon as the plate hit the table. She wondered what J.R. had to say now about her choice of career when just last month, he was cool with it. Lexi prayed that he didn't start tripping, especially since she was about to go hard at the club. She had to pay money to break the lease at the crib with Bre and find another place to live. She didn't have time to be arguing with his ass when all she wanted to do was make money.

Chapter 7

Alyssa spent the next few days relaxing in her home while surfing the web for Christmas gifts for her nephew Kyler and baby things for her new niece or nephew. She looked at a few things for her sisters and parents as well, as she thought about what everyone's plans were for Christmas. Thoughts of her returning home for Christmas crossed her mind, but she wasn't sure if that was something she would be up for. She planned on making things right, but having a face to face wasn't in the plan.

After a few days of relaxation, Alyssa woke up to her phone ringing at the crack of dawn and it was her boss telling her to be at the office by nine. Instead of rolling back over and going to sleep, she got out of bed, dragging herself to the kitchen to make her a quick breakfast. She filled up on cheese eggs, toast, and bacon before heading to the bathroom to handle her hygiene. As she got dressed in black pants suit, red blouse, and red ankle boots, she tuned into an episode of Maury where the husband was being accused of cheating on his wife with her best friend and she instantly thought about Anastasia. Alyssa hadn't reached out to her sister since they left to return home and she couldn't imagine what her sister was going through, but that bitch was definitely on her hit list.

Alyssa filled her Gucci purse with her wallet, phone, charger, and lip gloss before grabbing her coat and heading out the door. She used the remote to unlock her car doors and jumped inside. Grabbing her sunglasses out of its compartment above her head, she threw her shades on, cranked up her car, and pulled off. She arrived at headquarters minutes later and parked in a nearby spot. She grabbed her purse before locking up her car and swiping her badge to get inside. After the short elevator ride, she stepped off and saw one of her team members preparing coffee when she walked through the double glass doors. They made small talk about their holiday and discussed how they weren't ready to return to work as they walked to the conference room. Alyssa pulled her cellphone out her purse to put it on silent when she saw that she had a text from Corey.

Corey: Meet me at my crib later on tonight. We need to talk.

Alyssa: Okay.

Corey: I love you.

Alyssa: I love you, too.

She placed her phone on silent and tossed it back in her bag. Alyssa was glad that Corey texted her because her suspicions were starting to get the best of her. Thoughts of Corey cheating had entered her mind for the moment, but she quickly dismissed it. Alyssa viewed herself as cool, calm, and collected, but she would hate to have to kill the nigga she planned on spending the rest if her life with because he wanted to be stupid.

A few minutes later, the rest of the team entered the conference room and the meeting began. The chief presented new information and pictures of D'Mani Mitchell that was gathered over the holidays. The pictures showed D'Mani coming out of a house, a couple of traps spots, and getting in and out of few cars. Most of the pictures were taken at night, but the one that was taken in the day time caught her attention. She looked at the license plate to see if she recognized it, but she didn't. The car looked familiar to her like she had seen it somewhere before, but she couldn't remember where. The chief informed them that since their target was more mobile at night that they would have to be as well and Alyssa wasn't happy with that at all, but she didn't complain. They wrapped up their meeting an hour and a half later and they dismissed for the day. Alyssa pulled out her phone and took pictures of the photos of the cars and their license plates before she exited the conference room.

Alyssa stayed at headquarters looking through files trying to find something that would bring them closer to their target, but she came up empty. All they had on D'Mani was the basics and what they discovered about his past, which was that he was in and out of juvie and that he went from a petty thief to a drug lord damn near overnight. They just didn't know how he did it or helped him. After reviewing what she already knew about D'Mani, for the past couple of hours, Alyssa decided to call it a day.

Alyssa left the building and jumped into her car bringing it to life. She retrieved her phone from her bag and called Anastasia, but she didn't answer. So, she left a voicemail. She was worried about her sister and just wanted to know that she was okay. Thoughts of her parents entered her mind and she decided to call home. Plugging her earphones in, she called her mother as she backed out her parking spot and drove off. Her mother answered on the third ring.

"Well, hello Alyssa," her mother sounded surprised.

"I can tell by the sound of your voice that you weren't expecting to hear from me."

"After that stunt you pulled, no I wasn't."

"How's dad doing?" she tried to ignore her mother's attitude.

"He's doing better. He's sittin' in the livin' room watchin' television."

"Can you put him on the phone, please? I would like to talk to him."

"For what, Alyssa? So, you can send him back to the hospital?"

"Mom, I apolo-."

"Ever since y'all left, I've been thinkin' about where we went wrong with you girls. We did our best to teach you right from wrong and live by the word of God, but it seems like y'all discarded everythin' we taught y'all when y'all got grown. I can never understand how children can grow up in the same house and all turn out differently. Despite the fact that you almost killed your father, you don't even like your older or baby sister. What the hell has gotten into you?"

"Mother, I called to talk to dad and to apologize for the scene I caused at church. I didn't call to upset or argue with you, but I will say this... You say you've been thinking about where y'all went wrong with us. Well, how about you start at the beginning and you might discover where my dislike for my sisters began. Did you ever wonder why me and Anastasia are so close?"

Her mother remained silent.

"Mom, I love you and I will call to check on you guys again at another time and tell dad I love him, too."

Alyssa ended the call as she parked in front of her condo. She sat in her car for a few minutes and replayed the conversation she had with her mother. It broke her heart to hear how Victoria felt about her and her sisters. As badly as Alyssa wanted to lash out at her mother and tell her how her and Abraham basically divided their attention between Andrea and Alexis throughout their childhood, leaving her and Anastasia out of damn near everything and how their father forced Anastasia to marry a man that was cheating on her, she didn't. She took the high road and Alyssa was proud of herself for not making things worst.

Locking up her car, she unlocked the front door and walked inside where she saw a big bouquet of red and pink roses sitting on her kitchen counter along with I'm sorry balloons and shopping bags. Alyssa's mood immediately changed as she walked over to her gifts and smelled the roses. She removed the card from its holder and read what it said.

Tonight, it's all about you, Alyssa, and I'm sorry for rushin' out on you. Forgive me.

Alyssa squealed like a spoiled kid in a toy store. She knew that night was going to be something special and she couldn't wait to see what her husband to be had in store for her.

Chapter 8

It had been two days since Richard had given Anastasia his "proposition" and she still had yet to accept defeat, even after she'd spoken to nearly ten divorce attorneys who all told her that they would not take her on. There was no way that Richard had that kind of pull, not on his own anyway. He was obviously getting assistance in blocking her attempts at divorce, but Anastasia was not about to let him win. She still had a few tricks in her bag and if all else failed, she would most definitely get Andrea involved. That was the very last thing she wanted to do, but if push came to shove, she knew her sister would have her back if nobody else did; despite any of their issues.

The first thing she did was contact the bank, so that she could get Richard's statement for his black card. If he was the one that Lizz had been creeping with, then it must have been his card she was always bragging about having. It figured that low-budget hoe would be that thirsty to walk around using a card with the same name on it as Anastasia's, instead of being a smart side bitch and getting her own account. Lizz had been real bold messing with Richard and grinning in her face like they were cool, but now all of a sudden, she was ducking Anastasia like she owed her money. Richard must have told her that Anastasia knew about them because Lizz had been avoiding all of her calls since before she'd even left Mississippi. What Richard didn't tell her, Anastasia made sure to let her know on her voicemail though. She let her know that she was gone tag that ass as soon as she saw her. Just thinking about that hoe put a bitter taste in Anastasia's mouth and she felt herself getting pissed all over again. She couldn't wait till she got her hands on that bitch. If Richard thought that he was going to keep her in that stale ass marriage while he got his cake and ate it too, he had another thing coming.

Anastasia looked through the pictures that the private detective had sent her and rolled her eyes. See Richard thought that he was in control of all of their finances, but she was no dummy. Shortly after Kyler's first birthday, she'd opened up a bank account and had been depositing small amounts ever since, so that Richard wouldn't know. Her account wasn't anywhere near how much she had with Richard, but it was enough to hire a private detective.

After she'd left Richard's office and couldn't get ahold of D'Mani, she decided to take matters into her own hands. That dumb ass nigga never stopped fucking with Lizz, apparently, and the pictures in her hand proved it. Gathering everything together, Anastasia stood from her seat at their dining room table and prepared to leave and meet with the last attorney that she knew of. Their meeting wasn't for another hour, but she figured she would get a head start so that she wouldn't get caught up in traffic. She placed all of her things inside of her briefcase and headed out the door ready to get this over with.

She made it to the law offices of Abner and Roth almost forty-five minutes later. With her proof of Richard's affair in hand, she climbed out of her car and over to the building with her head held high. Just before she got to the revolving door, a text from Juanita came through stealing her attention and causing her to run smack into a hard chest. She looked up and locked eyes with Richard who wore a sinister grin. Immediately her mood soured and she couldn't stop the frown from spreading across her face.

"What are you doin' here?" she wanted to know, folding her arms across her chest to put some distance between them.

"You know why I'm here," he sneered and took a step closer, invading her personal space with ease.

"Did you really think that there was a lawyer in this city that I couldn't reach, Ana?"

She knew that his question was rhetorical, but a part of her still wanted to not give him the satisfaction of knowing that he had her in a corner. This was a new side of Richard that she wasn't used to seeing, being an aggressive person had never been his style. Or maybe it had and he'd just kept that part of himself hidden from her. She squinted her eyes at him, disgusted with what she saw.

"Yeah actually I did, but that's beside the point, Richard. Why do you even care so fucking much?" she asked angrily. It was mind blowing to Anastasia the lengths that he was going through to force her to stay in their marriage.

He frowned as he stepped even closer to her and grabbed ahold of her face.

"That mouth of yours has always been filthy, Ana…. but, as far as me caring… I've always cared. The way I see it, you're mine and you're always going to be mine." He looked over her face before she snatched away and he let out a chuckle.

"So, what you're sayin' is that we can't get a divorce because you feel some type of bullshit ownership over me?" she shook her head in confusion at what he'd just said. Richard had truly lost his damn mind if he thought for one second that he was going to leave her trapped in this fake ass marriage.

"Oh, it's not bullshit. I do own you sweetheart, but it's been two days since I gave you your only option and it's obvious that you decided against doing things my way. At this point, don't you realize that you're not gonna win this. I don't want this to get messy, but you keep pushing me.. Let this be the last time that I have to warn you though, Ana." he threatened and walked away, without giving her a chance to say anything. Anastasia stood there shocked and unsure about whether or not she should even still go up to see the attorney. Something told her it would be a wasted trip if she did, so with a deep sigh, she turned around and went back to her car.

Once she was inside the confines of her car, she let out a long, and loud scream. She was so frustrated that she didn't know what else she could do. On the one hand, she felt like Richard cheating was the push that she needed to leave, but on the other hand, she knew that the years she put in with him would have been a waste if she left with nothing. She knew that she needed to talk to D'Mani if for nothing else, for some reassurance that she was making the right decision. Before pulling off, she dialed his number only for it to go to the voicemail. D'Mani never had his phone off and the fact that she hadn't talked to him since she'd gotten back was really starting to bother her. After trying his phone a few more times just to be sure, she pulled away ready to pop up on him and see what the hell his problem was.

When Anastasia arrived at his house, she could clearly see D'Mani's car parked in his driveway with two others right next to it. Without getting out of her car, she called his phone again and surprisingly it rang a total of five times before his voicemail picked up once again. Her eyes burned with tears feeling as if he was ignoring her when she already was feeling so alone. The sound of laughter and loud talking drew her eyes up to his house and she witnessed D'Mani walking out of the house with some long weave wearing hoe at his side. Anastasia felt her face draw up into a scowl at the skimpy ass dress and cropped top the hoe had on. She watched as they played around in the driveway before he walked her to her car and they shared a deep kiss. He looked like he didn't even want to let her go when she pulled away from him and climbed inside of her car and pulled off after sharing a few more words.

Anastasia wiped her eyes, but the tears just kept coming, as she realized that maybe D'Mani had someone else that was willing to give him what she couldn't. Still her seeing him with someone else wasn't enough for her. Knowing that it probably wasn't the best idea, she wiped her face again and got out of her car and made her way up his driveway. When she reached the door, she rang the bell and tapped her foot impatiently waiting for him to come answer.

She could hear the locks turning and then there he stood looking even better than she last remembered. He was obviously about to get in the shower based on the towel draped around his waist. The confused expression on his face didn't go unnoticed, but that didn't stop her from talking.

"That's what we doin' now, huh? You havin bitches over here and shit, now?" she found herself shouting at him while he continued to just stand there looking at her with a raised brow. He seemed stuck on what she'd said without being able to form words to respond to her.

"I...I-.."

"No! I wasn't even gone a week and you already inviting hoes over here! You wanted me to rush and leave my husband and you doin your own thing anyway! Fuck you, D'Mani!" she cut him off and turned to walk away without letting him get in a word. She fumed the entire way to her car and the fact that he didn't call her back or at least try and stop her had her even more pissed off.

When she got inside, she started her car and looked back at the house to see him still standing in the doorway looking stupid, but he still didn't make an attempt to stop her. Here she was ready to give everything up to be with him and he was here entertaining other hoes. Still even with knowing that she might not end up with D'Mani, Anastasia was ready to divorce Richard. That was going to happen no matter if D'Mani wanted to be with her or not. There was no way that she was going to allow Richard to steal anymore of her life than he already had. Her heart pounded in her chest as she pulled away from the curb and dialed the only number that she knew she could at this point. The last thing she wanted to do was have to call Andrea, but it seemed like Richard was ready to stop anyone from helping her. She fumbled with her phone trying to dial her number and sat it in the seat next to her as the Bluetooth connected and the ringing filled her car. When her sister's voice came on the line, she took a deep breath as the tears kept falling.

"Drea......I need you."

Chapter 9

When Andrea left the doctor the day before, she went straight home and got in bed and thought about her life, scrolled through emails, watched TV, and thought more about her life until sleep found her. She thought that if she went to sleep and then woke up, things would be back to normal. Apparently, craziness was the new normal because as she sat at her desk the next day staring at her ultrasound, it still showed two little dots circled, one labeled A and the other B, signifying that she was pregnant with twins. Hannah seemed to be ecstatic, but to say Andrea was shocked and discombobulated would have been an understatement. Andrea had to figure out a way to tell her sisters, and then her parents, and Hannah was on her ass like white on rice demanding that she use her resources to find the mystery man from New York. She had called Lexi, but she didn't answer, and told herself to call Alyssa and Anastasia soon, just to check in on them. She had too much going on herself to still be upset about Thanksgiving.

Andrea couldn't worry about that at the moment because she had a case to win. The case that was scheduled for Thursday had been bumped up a day due to conflicting schedules. Andrea didn't really mind because she was already prepared, but had she not checked her email before she drifted off to sleep, she would have been screwed. She had about forty-five minutes before court was scheduled to start, and since she had a fifteen-minute drive, she gathered her things and headed out. Traffic was light, so she made it to her destination just like she had it mapped out in her head, which included her stop at Starbuck's. Drea parked and made her way inside, where she found her client as soon as she walked in.

"Good morning, Tanisha. How are you today?"

"I'm okay, Attorney Holiday, just a little nervous," she admitted.

"Why are you nervous? Everything will go fine and it's almost over."

"I can't help it."

"Just relax. You haven't done anything wrong, so this will be a no brainer," Andrea said after she took a sip of her Frappe.

The first thirty minutes were a breeze, but when Attorney Shields called his client, Kenyon Davis to the stand, things took an interesting turn the more he testified. The information that he disclosed hadn't been presented to Andrea, but it was his testimony and as long as the judge didn't allow the so-called tape that he mentioned to be entered into evidence, things would be okay. Andrea sat there trying her best to make sure that her facial expressions and body language weren't matching her mood, but she wasn't positive that she was succeeding the more she heard.

"I know it's painful, but can you explain to the court the events that led up to the night that you are speaking of?" Shields instructed his client.

"Tanisha approached me about spicing up our marriage. At first, it pissed me off, but I will do anything to please her... so, I finally agreed to it. We brought someone else into our marriage and I think that's what really ended it..."

As he talked, Andrea wrote a couple of questions down on her paper because she just heard the slip up in the testimony that should turn things back in their favor. Did you cheat first? Does he have a video? Did you cheat with the man you caught him with? She slid the paper to Tanisha and she shook her head no to the first question and yes to the second two when Andrea pointed to them. She was a little pissed off at her client, but she would find a way to get out of the hole. When Attorney Shields was done, she was given the chance to cross examine the witness.

"So, Mr. Davis, we're going to keep this short and sweet okay," Andrea smiled and he just stared at her with a grim expression and then nodded his head.

"So, you said bringing someone into your bedroom ended your marriage. Is that correct?"

"Yes ma'am. I believe that was what did it."

"Would your wife cheating on you not end your marriage?

"Yes… that's… that's what it was," he stammered.

"Earlier you testified about a video and said you caught her cheating first, then you later said bringing someone in was what did the detriment. Which is it?" Andrea questioned.

"Both," he said after a few minutes of silence.

"Is the man that your wife caught you with the same man that you two brought into your bed? If we allow this alleged video, will we see that?"

"Yes… I mean no. She cheated on me and now she wants half of what I worked hard for."

"Did she not keep the books at the business and was your business not a partnership?"

Andrea stared at him as he gave her a look filled with hate. Since he didn't answer, she continued and she was actually glad that things had taken a turn, but more thankful that her client whispered a few things to her during her soon to be ex-husband's testimony.

"Is it true that you became jealous of this man that you two brought into your bed because he appeared to be satisfying your wife better than you?"

"Fuck you and fuck her!! She's a whore and she's not getting my fucking money!" Kenyon jumped up and screamed.

"Order!! Order in the court!"

"No further questions, your honor."

Andrea sat down and released a deep breath. She felt Kenyon staring in their direction. It was to be expected, so she ignored him.

"If I ever represent you again, don't leave out any information," Andrea sternly whispered to her client.

"I'm sorry."

Andrea directed her attention back to the judge as she spoke. Kenyon jumped up and cursed the judge out as she made comments and was held in contempt of court. Andrea knew then that everything was just fine. It would be ninety days before everything was official and properties were broken down unless they reached an agreement that both parties would agree to. That would be farfetched considering the circumstances, but Andrea was cool with that. Her client was emotionally drained and she just wanted peace for her. When court was dismissed about ten minutes later, Andrea gave her clients instructions on what was next, and then she headed back to her office.

Almost an hour later, Andrea was walking back into her office with her plate from Piccadilly's. As soon as she sat down and took a few bites of her macaroni and cheese and pork chop, her phone vibrated. She looked at it and saw that it was Hannah texting.

Hannah: Have you found our baby daddy yet?

Andrea: You are such a fucking pest!!

Hannah: Bitch... that means you ain't did shit. Get a damn move on!

Andrea rolled her eyes and sighed. Once again, Hannah was right and she knew that she had to at least put forth an effort to find the man that had changed her life in more ways than one. She slightly smiled at the possibility of fucking the handsome and skillful stranger again, but that smile quickly vanished when she thought about the situation at hand. She was really pregnant by someone that she had a one night stand with. Un-fucking-believable. Andrea had connects everywhere, so she looked through her rolodex and retrieved a colleague in New York's information. After taking several deep breaths, Andrea placed a call to Felix.

"Well, what a pleasant surprise. What's going on, Ms. Holiday?" he answered after the third ring.

"Hey Felix... how's it going?

"Besides this freezing weather, everything is great."

"That woman must be mighty special to keep you up there in the big apple," Drea teased.

"She is… when you get ready to leave those woods, you should go ahead and come up here."

Brian was actually from Mississippi as well and graduated law school with Andrea. He wasted no time hauling ass from Mississippi and never looked back.

"Who knows… I just might surprise you soon… but listen... I need a personal favor."

"Anything for you."

Andrea explained everything to him of importance and felt confident that he would get the job done. Giving him the name of the hotel, the lounge, along with dates and times would allow any attorney to find information on anybody, and Felix was one of the best. She hung up, finished off her food, and then her phone began to ring. Noticing that it was Anastasia calling shocked Andrea, but she answered and was very surprised by the words that her sister spoke. Andrea dropped everything and went into protective mode for her sister.

Chapter 10

Lexi sat in the middle of J.R.'s bed, Indian style, going over her application for Graduate School before submitting it. She put in applications for Clark, University of Georgia, and Georgia State. Applying for a few schools back home in Mississippi crossed her mind, but when she looked at the time, she only had an hour before classes started, so that paperwork would have to wait until tomorrow. She closed her pink Mac laptop and scooted to the edge of the bed where she sat there for a moment just thinking. She had a lot on her plate and had someone told her that her life would be going in this direction, she would have told them that they were a fucking lie. Just as Lexi gathered her thoughts, her phone vibrated; she had an email from her school and she was pretty sure it was her final grades for the semester. Lexi wasted no time unlocking her phone and downloading the PDF file. Her eyes scanned over her grades as a wide smile spread across her face.

"Fuck you smiling for? What nigga texting you?" J.R. asked, walking up standing on the side of her.

"I ain't thinking about you or these niggaz...... BUT look!" she replied, holding up her phone, proudly showing him her grades.

Lexi got all A's in all four classes, a sense of relief came over her. Just when she felt like her life was falling apart, it was that moment she knew her hard work was paying off. She had one semester left and with a two -week break for Christmas, she was pretty sure that things would be a breeze.

"Aww shit! Look at you. Yo head ain't big as fuck for nothing," he joked, playfully mushing her upside the head before waking into his closet.

Lexi took a screenshot of her email and sent a picture to her mom as well as Drea. As soon as she pressed SEND, she called Drea since she still hadn't spoken with her since she got back to Atlanta.

"Well, it's about damn time," Drea fussed as soon as the call connected.

"I know…. I know" Lexi replied, rolling her eyes.

"Are you ok? Where you at? What the fuck was all that about the other day?" she asked, referring to when Lexi's phone accidently called her.

"I'm good, sister. I been staying with J.R.-"

"J.R.? ALEXIS!" she screamed into the phone.

"Chill Drea, I'm good! Did you get the message I just sent you?" Lexi asked, changing the subject.

Drea placed her on hold, so she could take a look and came back on the line screaming.

"That's what I'm talking about, Baby Holiday. I'm proud of you. Did you tell ma?" she questioned.

"I sent it to her when I sent it to you and thanks. I'm just ready for the shit to be over annnndddddd GUESS WHAT?"

"What?"

"I've applied for Graduate School." Lexi said excitedly.

"Baby Holiday, you just showing out. I guess it took for you to turn gay and strip in order for you to get your shit together," Drea teased.

Lexi knew her sister was only joking, so she didn't take her words to heart.

"I got something to tell you too though," she continued.

Lexi sat quietly and waited for her sister to spill the beans.

"I went to the doctor and I'm having twins!" Drea confessed.

Lexi screamed into the phone so loud that she caused J.R. to turn around and look at her crazy.

"Bittttccchhhhh!! OH MY GOD! I can't believe this. Let me go on Gucci right now to get my TT Babies some shit. You know them other hoes gon try to upstage me," Lexi ranted on.

"Wait. Wait. Slow down!" Drea laughed.

"Speaking of other hoes, your favorite sister is coming here for help," she continued.

"Favorite sister, my ass, but which one?" Lexi questioned.

"Stasia. She's trying to divorce Richard and he's giving her a hard time," she explained.

Lexi talked to Drea while she slipped on her clothes and prepared for school. They talked up until the time she walked into class. Lexi told her that she'll call her back tomorrow because she had to go straight to work after she left school. Of course, Drea sucked her teeth and ended the call on a bad note.

Lexi sat in her advanced accounting class taking notes, she'd usually be spaced out or on Facebook, but seeing her grades today actually motivated her. Professor Smith let them out ten minutes before class was over, which pissed Lexi off. She hated when her professors dragged the class along with little bullshit, it was mainly due to the same idiots who kept raising their hands asking dumb questions.

When she was released, she went straight to her car and headed to Blue Flame. She called Marcus and talked to him on the way there, filling him in on all the bullshit that was going on in her life. Marcus was the only person who knew about Bre's and Lexi love affair outside of them. He couldn't believe the shit he was hearing and made Lexi promise to call him when she left the club regardless of the time.

It felt like months had gone by since the last time she had been there, when in reality, it had only been a week. Although it was Tuesday, it was ladies' night, so that alone brought in a large crowd. When Lexi walked through the doors, everyone greeted her, including the bouncers, bartenders, the other dancers, as well as the regulars there. She acknowledged everyone and headed towards the back to the dressing room. Lexi went to her locker and put in the code before grabbing out the things she needed to take a quick shower. Once she was done, she put on her outfit, which consisted of a neon green thong and a bra that only covered her nipples. She had two performances tonight; the first one was in thirty minutes, therefore she had time to lay low and scope out the crowd.

"Well bitch, I thought you quit," Lexi heard a familiar voice say from behind her.

She turned around with a smile on her face at the sight of her work bff, Meka. Meka and Lexi started dancing at the same time and it seemed like they automatically clicked. Meka too went to Clark, but she dropped out their sophomore year and completely focused on dancing.

"I misssseeeddd yooouuuuu," Lexi sang, giving her a tight hug.

Meka squeezed Lexi's ass, causing her to laugh. The two of them sat in the dressing room and talked the entire thirty minutes up until it was time for Lexi's performance.

"I know y'all been looking for her, shiddddd I have too. Coming to the stage next is one of Blue Flames baddest women, y'all call her Sexy Lexi, but I'm trying to call her bae. Get ya money out and show my girl some love Atlanta!"

Lexi giggled at the way DJ Money announced her while she waited for her que to hit the stage. She looked over to her right and with a single head nod, the bouncer Reese gave her the signal and she took off.

> *I like it when you lose it*
> *I like it when you go there*
> *I like the way you use it*
> *I like that you don't play fair*
> *Recipe for a disaster*
> *When I'm just try'na take my time*
> *Stroke is gettin' deep and faster*
> *You're screamin' like I'm outta line*

Lexi's slowly walked onto the huge stage, her hips swaying to her every word Tank sang. The entire building erupted when she came from behind the red curtains. She sashayed over to the pole in the center and wasted no time

112

seducing the cold metal. Lexi slowly climbed to the top, while everybody in the building stood to their feet. They all looked on and waited for Lexi's famous "death drop".

When we fuck
When we fuck
When we fuck
When we fuck

On beat, Lexi dropped down into a split causing the speculators to go crazy. Twenty's and fifties were now covering the stage and Lexi got hyped at the sight of the money. She put on a show and two songs later, she was done. With the help from Reese, Lexi collected her funds from the night and exited the stage. While back in the back, she took another shower and threw on a pair of pink spandex shorts and the bra to match. She planned on making her rounds before her second set on stage.

Lexi scooped out the crowd again before heading towards the bar to get a shot of Patron. She held a brief conversation with the bartender before a guy in all black with a gold grill, caught her eye. Lexi and the unknown man locked eyes for a brief second before he motioned with his hand for her to come to him.

"Girl that's Magic; that nigga got a lot of money," Kitty the bartender whispered to her.

"I ain't never seen him before," Lexi replied.

"I heard he been laying low, he's been in here a few days since you've been gone. That nigga never requests anybody, you better go see what he want."

Lexi gulped down her second shot of Patron and made her way over to where Mr. Magic was. He gave off a small grin, displaying the house mortgage that he kept in his mouth.

"Sexy Lexi, huh?" he said with a smirk.

"The one and only. What could I do for you sir?" Lexi asked, slightly flirting with the fine ass specimen in front of her.

Magic licked his lips and opened his mouth to speak, but his eyes bucked and he shook his head instead.

"Nevermind shorty," Magic said before standing to walk away.

"That was weird," she mumbled to herself before turning around and colliding with a pissed off J.R.

"WHAT THE FUCK YOU DOING HERE?" he shouted.

"I'm at work and you need to lower your fuckin voice," she demanded.

"Didn't I tell you that you needed to quit this motherfucker?" he asked.

"First of all, you ain't tell me shit and second of all, you CAN'T tell me shit," she snapped.

"So, Lexi we ain't talk about this?" he asked, way calmer than a few seconds before.

"No, we did not. You said that we needed to talk about it, but we never got around to it," she explained.

J.R. stood there staring at her before finally replying, "My bad, but I meant to tell you that you gotta quit working here if we gon be together," he said nonchalantly.

Lexi laughed, "Boy you got me fuck'd up. BYE!"

She threw him the peace sign and tried to walk off, but he grabbed her arm and pulled her back.

"Look Lexi, I fuck with you the long way and at this point, I don't wanna lose you over something stupid," he stated.

"Stupid? My job stupid now? Since when?"

"Since I decided you finna be my girl. You don't need to do this shit," he explained.

"You gon take care of me, Jeremy?" she asked, placing both hands on her hips.

"Alexis, you would NEVER have to want for shit. I got you," he said sincerely, looking her in the eyes.

For the first time ever in her life, Lexi trusted the word of a man, she just hoped not to regret it later down the line.

Chapter 11

The evening that Corey had prepared for Alyssa was a beautiful one. The candle light dinner was romantic and the food was delicious. When they were finished eating, he swept her off her feet as they danced. The full body massage along with passionate love making made Alyssa forget what she was mad at him for. By the time she left his crib, they were back to being on good terms and he had her floating above the clouds yet again. She loved when everything was going right in her relationship. It kept her focused and improved her work ethic.

Now that her team was working at night, Alyssa spent most of her day at the office trying to get a lead on their case. She was tired of coming up empty handed. D'Mani was starting to become Mr. Untouchable, but that shit was about to come to an end. A couple of days after her dinner with Corey, she went into the office early that morning and got to work. Alyssa typed in the license plates of the vehicles from the photos and came up with a match for each of the cars. One belonged to a man and the other belonged to a woman. She wrote down the home and work addresses of the vehicle owners before she called Tara, the other female member on her team. Alyssa and Tara were recruited into the FBI together and since they were out-numbered by the four men on their team, Alyssa figured that they should work together on this case.

She picked up the office phone, dialed Tara's number and she answered on third ring.

"Hello!" she answered cheerfully.

"Hey Tara. It's Alyssa."

"Hey girl. I thought it was the chief calling me from the office. What you doing there? We're supposed to report to our locations at night. Did we have a meeting or something?"

"No, we didn't have a meeting. I'm working on our case. Which is the reason I'm calling."

"You got my attention."

"I just found the owners of the vehicles that were in the photos and I wrote down their information. I was going to check them out by myself, but being as though I can't be in two places at once and how we're somewhat overlooked, I wanted to know if you wanted to help me out with this."

"Hell yeah! You don't know how tired I am of not having anything to report to the team. I was starting to feel useless. I need to hang with you more often. Maybe I'll learn how to get ahead on this team."

"I hear you, but remember that we're still a part of a team, Tara," she chuckled.

"Now, take this information down."

"Okay, I'm ready. Wait, is the owner of the cars men, women, or both?"

"Both. Why?"

"I'd rather follow the woman if you don't mind."

"No problem. Here's the info."

Alyssa told Tara everything she needed to know and reminded her to follow the woman wherever she went and if she hooked up with D'Mani to take lots of photos of them and whatever they were doing. Tara agreed and thanked her before she ended the call. Alyssa logged off her computer, snatched up her belongings, and headed out the door. Hopping in her car, she googled the work address of the male suspect and found out that it was a club. It was still a little early and even though clubs weren't open to the public until late in the evening, the owners of the clubs would be there in the day time. Alyssa was about to head over to the club, but decided to go home and change her clothes. The skirt suit she was rocking would be a dead giveaway that she was the Feds.

When Alyssa got home, she changed into a white tee shirt, a pair of tight dark denim jeans, a tan waist length cardigan with a pair of wheat colored Timbs. She took her hair out of the tight bun letting it fall to her ass. Alyssa switched from her purse to her tan colored backpack, filling it with everything she needed. Grabbing a piece of fruit and a bottled water, she left out the house and headed over to the club. She called Corey to see if he made it to his destination safely, but he didn't answer. Alyssa figured he was still getting settled and couldn't talk at the moment.

Pulling up to the club a half hour later, she parked around the corner. Alyssa grabbed her phone before locking up her car and walking down the block. It was freezing in New York, but Alyssa switched down the street with no coat on like it was summer time. She pulled the door to see if it was open and it was. She walked inside and admired her surroundings. There were a few people inside cleaning up and taking inventory. Alyssa was about to get the attention of someone behind the bar until a man called out to her.

"Excuse me, Ma? Can I help you with somethin'?"

Alyssa damn near fainted when she turned around and saw that it was D'Mani Mitchell, her target, asking to assist her.

"Yes. I would like to talk to someone about booking a birthday party here for my sister?" She quickly got herself together.

"I can help you with that. I'm D'Mani, co-owner of the club," he said with an extended hand and a smile.

"Nice to meet you. I'm Amanda," she quickly lied.

"Follow me up to my office and we can start planning your party."

Alyssa followed behind D'Mani to his office and when they were inside, she admired the nicely decorated office and tried to spot anything out of the ordinary, but everything was clean. He sat behind his desk and Alyssa sat down and discussed the party packages and availability. After setting up a fake party for some time in February, Alyssa made a down payment before shaking his hand and getting up to leave. The office door flung open nearly hitting Alyssa, but she jumped back.

"Man, these motherfuckas gonna make me kill they asses if they fuck up this shipment," the man that nearly knocked her over spoke as he entered.

"Damn. My bad. I didn't know you had company, D." The six-foot two stranger licked his lips as he lustfully eyed Alyssa up and down.

"Miss Amanda just booked a party at our club."

"Is that right?"

"Yes, it is," Alyssa flirted.

"Thank you for ya business and if you need anything else for ya party, just hit me up and I'll make it happen." The stranger gave her his card.

"Thank y'all and I will. Bye." She waved before walking out the office.

As Alyssa closed the door, she heard Corey's name being mentioned and tried to listen as best she could.

"Yo, when is Corey getting' back in town? We need that nigga on our team permanently. He's the only nigga I trust when it comes to looking over the product."

"I hear you, but my nigga got a fiancée now. But, he just told me that he got caught up in a situation that he had to handle. His chick thinks he away on business, but this is more of a pleasure trip. You feel me?"

Alyssa walked off before someone caught her eavesdropping. She power walked out the club with her phone in hand. She called Corey again and it rung straight through going to voicemail. Alyssa walked to her car, hopped in, and sat behind the wheel for a minute as she thought about the conversation she just heard. She wasn't sure if they were talking about her soon to be husband, but with his sudden change in behavior and the week long break he took from her when he found out that she was an FBI agent, had her head spinning.

She hung around the club until D'Mani made a move a few hours later. The stranger that flirted with her and D'Mani hopped in the car with the same license plate that was in the picture. Alyssa followed behind them and took pictures of the stops they made and of D'Mani getting physical with one of his workers. When the stranger dropped him off at the chick's house, she saw that Tara was parked not too far from her crib. They made eye contact as Alyssa drove by Taras' car. After D'Mani went inside, Alyssa drove home. There was no need for her to go to her location because she knew where her target was and Tara knew what to do.

Alyssa grabbed her some food from Burger King before she arrived home. She walked over to her couch and turned on the TV. She flipped through every NBA and sports channel looking for Corey and he wasn't on either one of the channels. Alyssa became furious the more she thought about the situation. Corey avoided her for a week because she kept her job a secret from him, but his ass was probably keeping secrets from her. She continued to call Corey, but her calls went unanswered and when someone did answer, they would just breathe on the phone for a few seconds and hang up.

Besides the not being able to reach Corey, Alyssa was happy that she finally had some useful information on D'Mani. Hearing his partner talk about a shipment along with the pictures she took of them at one of the traps spots brought them closer to catching their target. She hoped that Tara would get more incriminating photos of him later on that night. Alyssa stayed up for as long as she could until she nodded off on the couch.

The next morning, Alyssa's phone was ringing off the hook and since her phone wasn't playing a special ringtone, she ignored the calls. Minutes later, her phone rang again and she snatched it off the table. When she saw it was Tara calling, she quickly answered the phone.

"Hey Tara."

"Giirrll! I caught D'Mani in the act of everything last night and some drama popped off with him this morning. I got pictures and everything! I'm on my way to the office now."

"Come to my house first, so we can look through the photos together, before we turn them in. I'm going to text you my address."

"Cool."

Alyssa texted Tara her address before she went into the bathroom to wash her face, brush her teeth, and change her clothes. The doorbell sounded throughout the house and Alyssa answered the door to let Tara in. Tara took a seat on one of the barstools at the island while Alyssa grabbed her camera out of her backpack and carried it over to the kitchen.

"This is a nice ass condo, Alyssa."

"Thanks girl." She smiled.

"You live her by yourself?"

"Yup. My fiancé spends the night some time." They swapped cameras.

"I wish I could get away from mine."

Alyssa looked at her with a raised eyebrow before returning her focus back to the camera. Alyssa was impressed with the pictures Tara had taken. There were photos of him with bricks of cocaine in his hand, him testing the cocaine with his tongue, and him giving his connect two duffle bags, which had money inside of them. She also had pictures of D'Mani placing duffle bags of cocaine into the chicks' car before she dropped him off at home. Tara followed the girl and took pictures of her as she dropped the drugs off to the trap spots and returned to D'Mani's house. Alyssa was about to hand Tara back her camera until a familiar face caught her attention. She quickly scrolled through the photos until she got a good look at the woman's face and her mouth hit the floor when she saw it was her sister, Anastasia.

"What the fuck is she doing at D'Mani's house?" she mumbled to herself.

"Did you say something?

"Huh? Oh, naw."

"Look, I'm going delete these photos because they're really not relevant."

"She could be a suspect as well."

"If she was important to the case, she would have been more involved in his day to day operations, Tara," she stated sternly.

"I'm deleting the photos."

Alyssa deleted the photos and handed Tara back her camera. She told Tara to print her pictures out and hold them, so that they could crack the case on their own and sent her on her way. Alyssa began to pace the floor as she thought back to the conversation they had when they had lunch together. *Was D'Mani Anastasia's side nigga?* Alyssa continued to pace the floor as a migraine began to brew. Between Anastasia being at D'Mani's house and Corey not answering his phone and possibly having a connection to D'Mani, she was about to lose it. Alyssa didn't know for sure if there was any connection between any of them yet, but if the two people she cared for the most had any ties to a Kingpin, she was going to have to make a serious decision between her career and her family.

Chapter 12

Anastasia looked over at a sleeping Kyler as they rode a redeye flight out to Mississippi. She was sure that she looked a hot ass mess from all of the crying and worrying that she'd done after running into Richard yet again, and then seeing D'Mani with another woman. The last twenty-four hours had drained her emotionally, and physically, but for Kyler's sake she knew that she had to muster up the strength to get through everything. After she'd called her sister damn near unable to get the words out, Andrea told her to come back home, so that she could see what her options were. She'd planned on leaving on the weekend, so that Kyler wouldn't miss any school, but unfortunately, Richard had called not too long after that saying that he wanted his son and he was coming the next day to pick him up. Anastasia had no intentions of letting him get ahold of their son after the threats that he'd made. She was already distraught, she didn't need to be worried about whether or not his ass was trying to kidnap Kyler. So, she left like a thief in the night with her son in tow and she didn't plan on coming back until her and Drea figured out a way to bring Richard to his knees.

Besides that drama, she had been avoiding D'Mani's calls. Whatever he needed to say he should have said that shit when she was standing in front of him crying her heart out. She knew at some point she would have to talk to him again, because no matter what she loved him, and she couldn't really fault him for wanting to have someone when she wasn't available. Still she couldn't stop herself from feeling hurt by it, and she finally understood how he'd been feeling the entire time. At that moment, she was just dealing with too much to try and fix things with him, and she could only hope that after she took care of her issues with Richard, they could work on their relationship.

The announcement for the end of the flight brought her out of her thoughts and she started preparing to get off of the plane. She was glad that she'd packed fairly light, so that she could manage her luggage and Kyler because he wasn't little anymore. Hoisting him up on her shoulder, she slung his carry-on into the crook of her arm and made her way through the small aisles, then off the plane. Surprisingly, the airport wasn't as crowded as she thought it would have been and she made it through baggage claim pretty quickly. She made it outside and grabbed one of the waiting taxi's in less than ten minutes. It was right on time too because Anastasia felt like her arm was about to fall off carrying around Kyler's dead weight. She gave the man Andrea's address and sat back in her seat with her eyes closed figuring she'd take a quick catnap for the trip since she hadn't gotten a wink of sleep during her flight.

"Miss.... miss we're here." The voice of the cab driver woke her from her sleep and she realized that she was in front of her sister's house.

She paid him the fair and gathered Kyler while he ran around and got her things out of the trunk. She followed him up the walkway to the door and gave him an appreciative smile before knocking. Thankfully, she'd texted her before their flight landed, so she was on alert and came to the door as soon as she knocked. Andrea was dressed in a pair of flannel pajama bottoms with her robe tied tight and her bonnet on.

"Come on in here," she said, opening the screen door and pulling in my luggage. "I'm glad you made it."

"Yeah, it was a pretty smooth trip." Anastasia smiled faintly shifting her weight to her other leg.

"Well, come on let me take you to the room you guys are gonna stay in cause I know this lil apple head boy got your arms aching," Drea joked causing both of them to laugh lightly, before leading her up the stairs and to one of her guest rooms. As soon as she saw the bed, Anastasia dropped her son's heavy ass down on it and sighed in relief.

"It's a bathroom in here and you guys have towels and extra toothbrushes if you need them. I'll let y'all get some sleep and then we'll talk everything over once you guys get up," Andrea said, heading back for the door.

"Thank you, Drea... I appreciate you helping me," Anastasia called out, stopping her before she left out of the room.

"We sisters girl, I'm gone always have your back." Drea smiled and ducked her head, walking out and closing the door behind her.

Anastasia couldn't help the smile that covered her face knowing that her sister was willing to help her out with no hard feelings about the past. She stood up and took off Kyler's clothes and shoes, before slipping off her own shoes and laying back on the bed. It didn't take her any time to fall asleep feeling a little more hopeful about things.

Anastasia woke up to an empty bed and realized that it was well after twelve in the afternoon. She figured that Kyler had hopped his ass up at about seven that morning and went and bothered Andrea once he realized where they were. Since it was so late, she hurried to get in the shower and handle her hygiene before dressing casually in some black, yoga pants and an off the shoulder maroon sweater. She slipped her feet into her house shoes, and made her way down the stairs where she heard Andrea and Kyler having a conversation. She couldn't help but smile at how much her sisters loved her son despite their differences.

Kyler spotted her before Andrea did who was dressed in some sweats and cooking some burgers with her back turned to them.

"Mommy!" he said, excitedly jumping into her arms. She hugged him back and gave him a quick kiss on the top of his head.

"Good afternoon sleepy head," Drea greeted her with a warm smile before turning back to the stove.

"Good afternoon, I must have been really pooped after that flight. I wanted to wake up earlier."

"Mommy said poop!" Kyler giggled, covering his mouth and making Anastasia roll her eyes at his silliness.

"It's okay, me and Ky were just catching up." Drea smiled and shrugged as she finished with the burgers and sat them on the countertop with all of the condiments to fix them up good.

"Yeah my baby's pretty good practice." Anastasia and her sister met eyes.

"Yeah, I guess I should be getting some practice in," Drea mumbled, before going to the refrigerator and bringing back a pitcher of Kool-Aid.

A silence fell over the kitchen as they both began to prepare their food. It was obvious that Andrea wasn't quite ready to talk about the whole baby thing, so Anastasia was okay dropping it at the moment, but she was going to want to find out how her niece or nephew was doing at some point during their trip.

"Soooo, how's dad been?" She wanted to know as she sat Kyler's burger in front of him and began to make her own.

"He's better, but it was a heart attack, so we're all just making sure that he's taking it easy......you might have known if you woulda stayed," Drea quipped and caused her sister to sigh loudly. Anastasia knew that it was coming, it wouldn't be Andrea if she didn't bring up something that she'd done wrong.

"I know Drea, it's just that it's a lot going on back home. I wanted to get a start on everything with Richard.... but, I'd rather talk about that later," she hinted and nodded her head in her son's direction as he stuffed his mouth with food.

Drea merely nodded, probably still feeling some type of way about them all leaving after their father collapsed in church, but she remained silent. Anastasia didn't want to argue with her sister or cause any tension either, so she suggested that they go and see their father after they finished eating and Andrea quickly agreed. It would give them a moment to talk without her son's prying ears and they could get a jumpstart on her situation. She knew that if anybody could help her it was Andrea and she needed her now more than ever. So, if visiting with their father would help, she was all for it; she just hoped that this entire trip wasn't a waste and that they could manage to get along, long enough for her figure out how to keep her son and her store. Anastasia didn't know how long their pleasantness towards each other was going to last, but she said a quick prayer that everything worked out and that her and her sister could remain on each other's good side for the next few days.

Chapter 13

It was Saturday evening and Andrea was sitting at her desk looking up information for Anastasia's divorce while she was out having some alone time and Kyler was in the living room watching *The Polar Express*. Andrea had talked to Lexi and spilled the beans about being pregnant with twins a couple of nights ago, but she had yet to tell her parents or other sisters. The shit still seemed surreal to her, but she decided that she would tell her parents and then, maybe she would do a four-way call with her sisters once Anastasia was back at home. As she thought about the four-way call, it made her think back to how every time they tried it, the shit took damn near an hour before everyone was on the phone, so they just texted instead. It never failed, Andrea would call Lexi, then Lexi called Alyssa, but every time Alyssa made the call to Anastasia, she hung up. Andrea laughed at the memories and decided that she would text them instead.

As she looked over everything that Anastasia had given her, she played around with a few ideas on how to handle Richard's bitch ass. For him to lock Anastasia out of her shop was weak as hell and Andrea was ready to jump on a flight to New York for round two of beating his ass. It wouldn't take much for her to call in a favor or two to get some documents back dated. Andrea didn't like to play dirty, but she had no choice when dealing with scumbags and would do anything for family. By Monday evening, she would have all of the information that she needed, but knowing exactly what Anastasia had and where she stood was helpful. Andrea made notes and a few questions that she needed to ask her sister. Instead of waiting on her to return, she went ahead and called her because she wanted to go next door and visit her parents shortly. Things were still tense between them, so Andrea only talked to her mom over the phone, but it was time for her to visit.

"Is Kyler okay?" Anastasia answered on the second ring.

"Kyler is fine… I just have a few questions."

"Oh okay… what's up?"

"The affair… Richard knows the name and everything?"

"Yep… he must have hired a PI or some shit," Anastasia guessed.

"Okay, we can approach this one or two ways… but, I suggest we act like you have no love connection with this man. We will only bring his name up IF Richard does, and with what I have in store for him, he probably won't."

"Okay… I just don't want him to get caught up in my bullshit with Richard."

"You love this man, huh?"

"I really do… I should have left Richard when he asked me," Anastasia sighed.

"Awww… well hopefully you two can be together when we get you away from this bitch ass husband of yours."

Andrea and Anastasia talked for a few more minutes until Anastasia ran into someone that she knew and hung up. She made a few more notes of a few loophole's to inquire about and sent Felix an email. Thank God he was a genuine friend or she would owe him big time. The thing about it, she would do anything for him too, so she knew that he didn't mind helping her out at any time. Once she was done, Andrea got up and went to check on Kyler.

"You wanna walk with me next door, nephew?"

"Do I have to? I would like to finish watching this if I can."

"Sure, you can... I'll be right back. I'm gonna lock the door and I'll use my key to come back in okay."

"Okay auntie," he replied and tuned back in to the TV.

Andrea smiled at her nephew's accent. She grabbed her North Face jacket from the coat hanger that was by the door, slipped it on and headed out after grabbing her keys and locking the door. It felt like she was doing the walk of shame for some reason, but Drea kept moving forward. It wasn't dark yet, so she didn't have to use her key to unlock the door because her mom hadn't locked it yet. When Andrea walked in, no one was in the living room, so she made her way to kitchen where she found her mom washing a few dishes and talking on the phone. The phone wasn't even on speaker, but she heard her Aunt Shirley's voice loud and clear.

"You know I don't care much for Abraham's prude ass, but I hate to see him going through this, and it's taking a toll on you."

"Shirley, I'm fine... we get the results back..." Victoria started saying, but stopped when she looked up and saw Drea.

"Let me call you back, Shirley. Drea just walked in."

"Tell Drea I want a baby named after me!"

"Bye Shirley!!"

"Hi mom. What you and Aunt Shirley talking about?"

"Hi Drea... you finally decided to come and check on your old folks in person?" her mom said and ignored her question.

"Mom... it's not like I didn't want to. It's been kinda awkward since... you know."

"You can't even say it," her mom sighed.

"Since y'all found out I was pregnant. I'm pregnant, mom... do y'all want me to have an abortion or something?"

"Andrea Holiday!! You better watch your tone!"

"I didn't come here for a confrontation, mom. I really just wanted to check on you guys. Where's dad?' she asked as she turned around.

"He's sleeping right now."

"Okay... I'll see y'all at church tomorrow!" Drea announced and made her way back towards the front door.

"Wait Drea... I need to talk to you about that."

Drea turned back around and tried to meet her mother's eyes, but her mom looked down. She knew that she was about to say something bad just by the way that she was fidgeting with her apron and not making eye contact.

"What's wrong, mom?" she quizzed.

"You're expected to make a public apology to the church."

"For what?"

"For having a baby out of wedlock. It's a sin."

"Do people make public apologies for having premarital sex? Or gossiping? Or overeating? Whose idea is this?"

"Well... it's a public sin and some of the elders at the church have spoken on it."

"I'm not doing that, mom. I don't owe anything to the elders of the church. God knows my heart!"

"Your dad expects it, Drea."

"I'm sorry mom... I'm not doing that. I love you guys more than I love myself, but I'm not apologizing to a church full of people who sin worse than me. I guess I won't be attending church." Drea turned and left with tears streaming down her face.

Chapter 14

Anastasia was in a better mood since arriving back home. Surprisingly, Drea had been extremely understanding and not as bitchy towards her as she expected her to be. She'd even volunteered to watch Kyler for a little bit, so that Anastasia could go out and get some time to herself, which is where she was headed right at that moment. She said her good-byes to her sister and Kyler and closed the door behind herself. The change in the temperature compared to New York allowed Stasia to only leave out with a jean jacket on. She straightened out her clothes as she walked to Drea's car with the keys swinging in her hands. She had been so excited about the opportunity to get some alone time, that she hadn't even figured out where she was going to go. Honestly, she didn't care where she went as long as she was able to just get some time to get her mind off of her own drama.

Once she was inside of the car, she started it up and sat scrolling on her phone trying to find something that she could get into. She started looking through what movies were currently playing when a tap at the window damn near made her drop the phone. Looking up she saw her Aunt Shirley standing with one hand on her hip and the other holding her flask up, motioning for her to open the door. Anastasia wondered where the hell she had come from considering her Mama and Daddy should have been resting. She rolled her eyes and hit the unlock button so that her Aunt could get in, instantly getting a whiff of whatever strong brandy that she was sipping on.

"Took yo ass long enough!" she huffed, getting comfortable in her seat and taking a sip of her drink.

"Sorry Aunty, it took me a second to realize who it was," Stasia lied, knowing that her Aunt wasn't going to believe her. She didn't miss the look on her face letting her know that she did in fact know that Stasia was lying.

"Mmm hmm." Aunt Shirley gave her the side-eye.

"When did you get back out here and why in the hell you sittin out in the car? Hidin from Drea?" she teased. Anastasia fought hard not to roll her eyes at the bull that was coming out of her mouth.

"Ain't nobody hidin from Drea, Aunty, Dang! I actually came because I needed her help with something."

"Mmph, I know Ms. Big City don't need her lil country sister help!" she paused long enough to take another sip and burp before she continued. "Richard must be givin' you a hard time with that divorce, huh?"

Anastasia's eyes bucked and she looked at her Aunt surprised that she knew her business without her saying anything.

"What? Yo Aunty know some stuff hell! You knew that nigga wasn't gone be tryna let you go so easy," she stated, matter of factly.

"Well, unfortunately he is tryna fight me on the divorce," Anastasia sighed heavily feeling a burden off of her shoulders after finally saying it out loud to someone else.

"He's threatening to take Kyler and my store."

"That muthafucka! You want Aunty to go lay his ass out? Seems like that beatin' you and yo sister's put on him wasn't enough," she fumed, bouncing around in her seat obviously getting amped up.

"Naw, Drea's figuring everything out now, that's why I'm here."

"So, where the hell you was bouta go? Let me find out you got a nigga out here…. do he got a uncle or a daddy?"

She gave her Aunty a stale face and shook her head stiffly.

"Naw, I ain't meetin no damn man. That's what got me in this mess in the first place. Drea's watching Kyler so I can get a minute to myself, so I was gonna just go and catch a movie." Aunty Shirley clutched her chest and drew her body back against the door like what her niece had just said was crazy.

"You got some time to yo self and you wanna go to the show?" she asked with a frown.

"I would say yo ass need a drink. Let's go catch Applebee's for them dolla' margaritas!" she motioned for Anastasia to go and she did just that. Stasia hadn't even considered taking a drink and now that her Aunt had brought it up, she knew it was just what she needed.

They pulled up to the Applebee's shortly after and Anastasia was more than ready to get out of the car. The whole ride Shirley's ass had been singing all loud and messing up the lyrics to all the damn songs. She hoped that her Aunty didn't act a fool inside of the restaurant because she didn't feel like being a baby sitter. Stasia walked ahead of her Aunty as she staggered to the door talking shit and cussing up a storm.

"Don't be tryna leave me girl!" she fussed, finally catching up to Anastasia at the hostess's desk.

"I wasn't tryna leave you Aunty," Stasia sighed and motioned for a table for two as Shirley grumbled and continued to talk shit behind her. The hostess smiled in understanding and led them to a booth, then handed them both a menu.

"What would you ladies like to drink this evening?" she asked, still smiling.

"Bring some margaritas and keep them bitches comin!" Anastasia nodded, so that the hostess could see that she wanted the same thing and the girl skipped away.

"Aunty Shirley, don't be cussin at these people like that," she scolded before lifting up her menu and scanning to see what she wanted to eat.

"Girl, ain't nobody worried about what come out my mouth, that's the beauty of old age." She shrugged just before the girl returned with their drinks. Aunt Shirley wasted no time digging into hers while Anastasia sipped her drink slowly.

"Mmm… this is pretty good."

"Naw, it ain't strong enough." Aunt Shirley claimed, shaking her head and pouring some of the brown liquor from her flask into her cup.

Anastasia frowned up her face as she watched her Aunt take a drink, then smack, and add another splash to the cup. Shaking her head Anastasia stood up.

"I gotta go to the bathroom, Aunty. I'll be right back."

She walked off without giving her Aunt a chance to say anything and hurried into the bathroom as if she really had to go. The real reason she wanted to get away from her

Aunt was because she'd noticed that she had missed a few calls and knew that they were from Richard. She'd already basically kidnapped their son, and the last thing she needed was to try and have this conversation in front of her drunk ass Aunty.

As soon as she hit the door to the women's restroom her phone buzzed again indicating another call from Richard. Anastasia took her time answering, so that she could get herself together, and then swiped across the screen. "Why are you blowing my phone up, Richard?" she demanded as soon as the call connected.

"You know damn well that I was supposed to be picking up Kyler, Ana! Well, I'm at the house right now and all of the lights are off. So, where the hell are you at with my boy?" he growled into the phone and she could tell that he was pissed. Really, she wanted to laugh at how angry he was, but she knew that wouldn't be a good idea. Maybe those margaritas were a little stronger than she thought.

She cleared her throat to stop the laugh that tickled there and put on her stern voice. "Wellllll, obviously we aren't home, Richard! Why don't you take yo ass somewhere else, like hmmm maybe that hoe Lizz's house! Oh, wait I forgot that hoe married like you are!"

"Ana, I'm not playin' with you! Where's my son?"

"That's for me to know and you to find out," she said, finally letting out a chuckle at how mad he was becoming.

It served his ass right for putting her through so much hell this past week. How did he think it was okay to threaten to take Kyler away from her? Then, it hit her that he hadn't expected for her to put up a fight. It was just like

Richard to assume that things would go his way, but he should have known by now that with Anastasia, he wasn't always going to get what he wanted.

"Listen, I've been about as civil as I can, but if you keep pushing me, Ana, it's not going to end well for you..."

"Why!? Because you gone take my business and my son! That doesn't scare me anymore Richard. You been sayin' that and I ain't worried!" she made sure to use the word "ain't" to further piss him off, loving the way she was handling herself this time around. Even if it was just over the phone.

"If you don't bring me my son back, I can promise you that you won't ever have to worry about anything ever again bitch!" he roared, causing the smile on her face to fall right off.

"Was that a threat?"

"I would consider it to be more of a promise Anastasia... and you know I get what I want! Let this be the last time I have to tell you to bring him to me... or else!"

Anastasia stood with her mouth wide open in shock at the man that she had spent the last six years of her life with. She wasn't sure if being with Lizz had turned him into a demon or if it had been there all along, silently waiting to show its face, but she couldn't lie and say that she wasn't scared to death. The phone beeped in her ear indicating the end of the call and she hurried to put it away, and then turned to face herself in the mirror. With trembling hands, she turned the water on and splashed some on her face hoping to erase the worry that was etched across it after that phone call. She stayed in the bathroom for a few more minutes trying to collect herself before going out to face her Aunt. She planned to block Richard's crazy ass as soon as she got back to the house and told Andrea about the conversation. After she gathered herself, she made her way out of the bathroom only to run straight into a hard chest.

"Well damn… if it ain't Anastasia Holiday." She heard that familiar voice and looked right into the eyes of Zyree. He was looking just as good as ever dressed down in a white screen tee and dark wash denim jeans, with some brown AKG boots on his feet, and God did he smell even better than he looked, if that were possible.

"Hello Zyree, how are you?" she asked, hoping to keep their conversation brief. She already had a crazy ass husband fighting her for a divorce and a thugged out ass side-nigga that she hadn't figured out things with. Her plate was literally full, and Zyree was standing before her looking like a whole snack that would surely cause more problems.

He smiled down at her from his height of 6' and pulled her in for a hug.

"I'm good, I'd be better if I hadn't let you get away, but I gotta feelin that's not gone happen again," he stated bluntly, pulling away just enough to look her over without releasing her.

"Why don't you let me get yo number so we can catch up."

"Look Zy, I'm married, with a five-year-old kid, okay?" Anastasia explained and wiggled out of his arms to flash her ring.

"So, no I can't give you my number." The look on his face was one of confusion and sadness, but what quickly replaced with a neutral expression.

"So, you really went ahead and married that nigga, AND gave him a shorty?" Anastasia almost felt bad about the hurt that laced his voice, but he had made his choice years ago and in turn she had made hers also.

"I actually did. It was great running into you though," she tried to lighten the mood before they parted ways, but it didn't seem like that was going to happen.

"I'll see you around though, right?" He wanted to know as she walked away.

She didn't want to leave him there like that. At one point, she had loved that man and would have easily chosen him over Richard any day, but if that was the case, she wouldn't have Kyler. Without turning around, she shook her head no and continued to her table hoping that he just dropped the whole thing. When she got back to her table, Aunt Shirley was on her third drink, because apparently, she had drunk her own, drank Stasia's, and ordered another one.

"Mmm hmm... you ain't slick. Dip yo ass off to the bathroom and take all that time, then come back and got some nigga all in yo face! Yo sneaky ass went and got some bathroom sex!" she cackled, squinting her eyes at her.

"Ain't nobody get no sex, Aunty. Now, why did you drink my drink?"

"Cause, it was gone melt, duh! I ain't want yo money to go to waste."

She said it like it was no big deal. After rolling her eyes, Ana signaled to their waitress to bring her another margarita over. With all of the things she'd just dealt with in the last few minutes she was gone need a couple of them. Once the waitress acknowledged her request, she busied herself with looking around, and saw Zyree make his way back to a table where a cute dark-skin lady was waiting for him. That nigga had some nerve trying to come at her when he was there with a whole woman.

"You ain't getting off that easy, Stasia. Who is that nigga?"

Anastasia turned back to face her aunt and shrugged.

"Nobody important. Nothing for you or me to worry about."

"Mmph, well, nobody important sholl look like yo five-year-old son, but that's all I'ma say about that," Aunt Shirley said before drinking her margarita like she hadn't just threw major shade at her niece.

"Kyler is not his baby! And you better not say that to anybody else."

"Oh, you tellin' me what I bet not do? I'm the Aunty and you the niece. Don't get beside yo self and get that ass whooped, girl. I'm just stating the obvious."

Anastasia remained quiet as she thought about how people would love to carry that bone back to her father. If people thought that he was up in arms about sex out of wedlock, she could imagine how he'd react to finding out she'd committed adultery and in his eyes, had a bastard child. She could feel a headache coming on from just the thought and hoped that her Aunt wouldn't bring that up.

The last thing she needed on top of a divorce was a nasty paternity suit. Anastasia prayed that things didn't get any worse, but it just wouldn't be right if it didn't involve drama and the Holiday family.

Chapter 15

Lexi knew that one of the key ways to a man's heart was to be submissive and that's exactly what she did, submitted when J.R. demanded she stopped dancing. A few nights ago, she walked out of Blue Flame hand and hand with her man and hadn't been back since then. She was no fool though. The very next morning, she hit up Cooley, the owner of the club and told him she was taking a short leave of absence. In J.R.'s mind, Lexi quit, but the truth was, if she hadn't allowed her own parents to stop her cash flow, what makes you think, she'd allow a man to. Lexi went along with the idea truthfully for her own good. She had so much shit going on, she needed to get herself together. Dealing with her father's health, the uncertainty of her future and Bre's big head ass, she was feeling lost. She had more than enough cash to chill out from stripping for a few weeks and that's what she planned on doing; especially, since J.R. claimed he had her back.

Lexi sat in front of Marcus's house and blew her horn for what seemed liked the hundredth time. She then grabbed her phone out of the cup holder to FaceTime him. As soon as she reached his name in her contacts, he came skipping his chubby ass down the stairs.

"Bitch, you almost got left," she yelled, as soon as he opened the car door.

"Honey, perfection takes timmmmeeee!" Marcus replied, buckling his seat beat.

Instead of responding, Lexi laughed and pulled away from the curb. Seeing how her and her now only best friend hadn't spent any quality time together since she'd been back, she figured they'd go out to eat and catch up. Although they talked every day, she still had so much to fill him in on. Lexi headed to the Hooters on Peachtree Avenue, ready to smash some buffalo shrimp and vent to Marcus. She even planned on getting a margarita or two to calm her nerves.

"Marcus, can you look inside my wallet and make sure I put my ID in there? I plan on getting slightly tipsy and Imma be pissed if I left my shit in my other purse," Lexi stated.

Marcus did as she requested and went inside her Gucci purse, pulling out her Gucci wallet, fumbling through the contents inside.

"Ain't no ID, baby." he said, stuffing everything back.

"FUCK!" Lexi screamed, hitting the sterling wheel.

"Calm down, hoe. I got my ID. You can have a sip of my drink," he replied.

Lexi looked at him out of the corner of her eye.

"I ain't sharing shit with you. I'm about to stop and get my own shit," Lexi said, making a right at the very next light.

Lucky for her, she had to pass J.R.'s house in order to get to the restaurant anyway, so she wasn't tripping. Lexi and Marcus cruised the streets of Atlanta, listening and singing along to Destiny's Child's first album *Writings on the Wall*. That album took her back to when her and her first love, Miko, was rocking hard. Lexi smiled to herself and shook her head. She was so young and dumb back then, she was just glad she could laugh about it now. Just as Lexi's best Beyoncé impersonation brewed, her phone rang through the speakers. Her eyes darted to the dashboard,

Aunt Shirley's name flashed across. Lexi hit the button on the steering wheel, connecting the call.

"Yooooooo," Lexi yelled, causing Marcus to laugh.

"Yooooooooooooo," Aunt Shirley replied back, adding a few extra O's at the end.

Lexi and Marcus laughed out loud this time, Aunt Shirley was a mess but Lexi loved her to death.

"What's up, lady?" Lexi asked.

"Girrrlllll, you need to come back home. You missing it all," Shirley mumbled into the phone.

Although Lexi understood what she said, it was clear that her auntie was either drunk or on her way.

"What happened?" Lexi's interest was piqued.

"Why you ain't tell me that Richard ain't that baby's daddy?"

"Wait... Auntie, WHAT?" Lexi asked.

"Richard ain't Kyler's dad," she responded with so much confidence.

Lexi laughed again, it was at that moment that she knew Shirley was crazy.

"What are you talking about? That is my nephew daddy regardless of how much we hate that bitch. Unfortunately, Richard's weak, lame, limp dick ass is that baby's, Papa," Lexi assured her.

"You a motherfucker lie. I saw that boy real daddy. His name Tyree."

"ZYREE. Auntie do you mean ZYREE?" Lexi quizzed.

"Zyree, Tyree.... It's all the same."

"How you figure?" Lexi questioned.

"I seen him and he looks just like Kyler. This whole time the family thought you was the hoe and here it is the married sister. I couldn't wait to tell you so you could redeem your hoe points and pass them son of bitches right to Anastasia."

Lexi was laughing so damn hard that she almost drove pass J.R.'s house. Aunt Shirley continued talking but Lexi zoned out when she pulled into the driveway and noticed a female on the porch, talking to J.R.

"I swear to God, I'll kill this nigga," Lexi said aloud to no one in particular.

"Kill who? Lexi, it ain't that serious. You can't be doing no time behind him. Matter of fact, I can give you some pointers on how to get away with murder, but not on this phone. You know my phone might be tapped. Ya fuckin sister an FBI agent and shit.... All you hoes fucked up," Shirley ranted.

"Yeah, yeah, yeah, let me call you back," was all Lexi said before ending the call and putting the car in park, her eyes never left J.R. and his guest.

Marcus eyes darted back and forth from Lexi's and the porch before he finally put all the pieces together.

"Don't do ittttt," he said, unbuckling his seat beat, but it was too late, Lexi was already out the car and walking towards the house.

"It's cold as fuck out here, let's take our company inside Jeremy," she said, walking up placing both hands on her hips.

"Come on mannnnnnnnnnn" J.R. replied, throwing both hands up in the air.

"Did I miss something?" the unknown female asked.

"Who the fuck is this?" Lexi snapped. "Better yet, WHO THE FUCK ARE YOU?" Redirecting her question now to the female, while pointing her finger in the chick's face.

"I'm Amber and J.R, you wanna tell her who I really am because if I do, I might hurt the young bitch feelings."

Lexi turned around, and then stepped off the porch, looking down the street.

"What is you doing? Who you looking for?" J.R. questioned.

"I'm looking for the person this bitch talking to," Lexi replied, walking back up, that time stepping into the girl's face.

J.R. stepped down and stood in between the two. Lexi looked over and noticed Marcus switching from the car, swinging his knife around in the air. She wanted to laugh because that fool never left the house without Lucy, as he liked to refer to his weapon.

"Best friend do we have a problem here?" he asked, smacking his lips loudly.

"Nah, as soon as J.R. explains to me why shorty on his porch, then we can bounce," Lexi informed him.

"Look baby, this Amber. Amber popped up over here because I cut her off. We are standing out here because I ain't letting her ass in my crib," he explained.

"Ohhhh, so Amber, you stalking my nigga?" Lexi smiled, turning towards her.

"Wait, this the bitch that got you acting funny towards me?" Amber asked J.R.

Without warning, Lexi reached around J.R. and punched Amber, catching the bridge of her nose.

"I'm not finna be too many bitches," Lexi screamed while Amber jumped around trying to get to her, but J.R. wasn't having it.

"This how you finna do me J.R.? After all the shit we been through. Five years J.R.? Five years, huh? Over some lil young bitch," Amber screamed.

"Young BAD bitch. Please don't forget the BAD!" Marcus said, giving Lexi a high-five.

J.R. looked over at Lexi and Marcus shaking his head.

"Look Amber, you need to go. You got my shorty thinking I'm out here bad."

Amber took the back of her hand and wiped her nose before turning away and leaving. The three of them watched her get inside her car and pull off. Once she was out of sight, Lexi looked J.R. up and down before she too walked off.

"Where the fuck you going?" he asked, grabbing her by the elbow.

"Away from here. You got me so fucked up," she replied.

"FUCKED UP! I AIN'T EVEN DO SHIT! Look, you not finna leave me mad; we finna sit down and talk about this shit," he said.

"I can't. Me and Marcus finna go to Hooters," she explained.

J.R. snatched Lexi's keys out of her hands and threw them at Marcus.

"Big homie, gone to Hooters and bring me back some crab legs," he ordered.

Without saying a word, Marcus turned around and walked off.

"Nigga, you just gon leave me?" Lexi asked.

"Hell yeah, I'm finna ride through the block my lil boo be on. He gon see me in this Benz and want me back.... BYE BITCH!" Marcus said, leaving the two of them standing there.

Lexi hesitantly walked into the house behind him, taking a seat on the couch. J.R. grabbed a bottle of water out of the kitchen before taking a seat next to her.

"So, you really mad about that shit?" he asked, turning up the bottle.

"Nah, I just don't like surprises," she replied dryly.

"Surprises? You think I'll have a bitch in the crib that I share with you? I take all my hoes to the hotel now," J.R. joked, but Lexi didn't crack a smile.

"Awwwww... baby come here," he said, pulling her close to him.

"On some real shit, I wouldn't do no shit like that. When I first started talking to you, I told you that I don't have time for bitches. You a hand full by yourself, a nigga can't cheat if he wanted to, but you gotta know that I have a past and with having a past, I have exes. But, I'm only rocking with you," he explained.

Lexi wasn't sure if she believed him or not although she wanted to, it was hard. He was right about the things he said, we all did have a past.

"J.R., what is it that you do for a living?" Lexi blurted out.

It was obvious that her question caught him off guard by the look on his face.

"Where that come from?" he asked, scratching his head.

"The money. The way the dude at the club looked like he seen Satan himself when you walked up. Jeremy, you have a gun stashed away in damn near every room in the house. At first, I thought it was dealing drugs, but there's never any trace of it around. So, I pose the question again, what is it that you do?"

J.R. sat up straight on the couch and stared into space for a while. Lexi knew he was wondering whether or not he should tell her the truth.

"I don't have a title to give you, Alexis," he finally replied.

"Ok, fuck a title, give me the job description then," she insisted.

"I put in work. Most niggaz look at me scared and stay clear of me for a reason..."

"And that reason being?" she asked, cutting him off.

"Lexi, I kill niggaz for a living. If a motherfucker need me to put in work, I put in work. I make hits," he explained.

"So, you a hitman?"

"Nah, I ain't no motherfucker hitman," J.R. laughed.

"I don't find shit funny and according to your job description, that labels you a hitman."

Lexi could tell that JR was getting frustrated, but she needed to know what type of shit she was dealing with. Yeah, she was attracted to thugs, but if what JR was saying was true, he was a different type of thug.

"Listen, I run a business and employ a lot of ruthless niggaz. When I was a shorty, I didn't have the best upbringing. I was a lil rough nigga running the streets bad. Me and my cousin, Donnie, started robbing candy stores and then, we eventually graduated to jewelry spots by the

152

time we were teenagers. Never getting caught, we felt like we were invisible. One day, one of our hits went wrong and I had to pop a nigga who wasn't willing to give up his possessions. I saw how easy it was to kill him; I got accustomed to the shit. Me and Donnie had an idea of expanding our business, so we hired other young ruthless nigga from the hood who ain't have shit to lose, but had dreams of being rich. About two years ago, word got out that we were responsible for a lot of the killings and dealing going around in Philly, so I relocated. We still got a team on the East Coast, that Donnie's running and I'm handling shit down south. It's way more to it, but this all you need to know right now," he said, standing to his feet and walking out the living room.

"J.R.!" Lexi screamed out to him.

"As long as you with me Lexi, you are safe and will be well taken care of. I GOT YOU!" he yelled from upstairs.

Lexi flopped back down on the couch and folded her arms across her chest wondering what the fuck she had gotten herself into.

Chapter 16

It was hard for Alyssa to focus after she saw the pictures of Anastasia at D'Mani's house a few days back and Corey's name being mentioned in a conversation between her target and his partner. She spent the rest of that day blowing Corey's phone up. which was something she never had to do. When he finally answered around seven that evening, it took everything in Alyssa not to snap on him like she wanted to, but she managed. She played the role of a concerned wife instead of a bitchy one and even though he didn't tell her much over the phone, he promised that when he returned on that weekend, that he would explain everything to her.

The meeting that took place on Friday at the FBI headquarters was the same as usual, but the information about finding out who the vehicles belonged to and finding out that D'Mani was co-owner of a club piqued the interest of the chief. Alyssa informed the chief that she asked Tara to help her get intel on the female owner of the vehicle, but was blindsided when Tara presented photos to teams. Alyssa quickly scanned the photos and exhaled when she saw that the pictures she tossed on the table were of the girl she followed and not Anastasia or D'Mani. After a job well done from the chief, Alyssa pulled Tara to the side and questioned her about the pictures. When Tara explained to her that she felt that they should turn in some of the photos to kill suspicion, Alyssa agreed, but told Tara to give her a heads up next time.

Once the duo discussed their next move, they figured since it was still early that they would go to lunch to pass some time. When they arrived at The Modern, they were instantly seated by the hostess. Alyssa was curious about her partner and wanted to find out more about her without being too obvious. When they ordered their appetizers and drinks, Tara willingly began to open up. She expressed that she was unhappy with her life and that she was ready to break free from the grasp of her fiancé. Tara had been with him for a few years and a relationship that seemed to start out great took a turn for the worst when she discovered that her man had an outside baby. When she packed her shit to leave, she was exposed to his abusive side and been trapped ever since. After Tara finished up her story, Alyssa felt bad for her team member and wished that she could help any way she could.

After their lunch date, Alyssa went home and chilled for the rest of the day. She thought about how she hadn't talked to her favorite sister since they returned home for the holidays. She made a mental note to cuss her ass out the next time she saw or talked to her. Anastasia was already on her shit list for being at D'Mani's house and she needed answers ASAP. Alyssa made herself a pitcher of margaritas and drunk the night away as she thought about Corey and what the hell he was up to. She was thinking of all the possible things he could've been doing at the moment and what his connection to D'Mani was.

Alyssa woke up to use the bathroom and when she was about to get out of bed, she heard someone moving around in her living room. She snatched her gun from underneath the pillow, took the safety off, and got out of bed. With her gun aimed, she walked quietly down the hall. As she neared the living, she saw the person moving around and let a shot off.

"Don't take another fucking step!"

"Lyssa, cool the fuck out. It's me!"

Alyssa quickly flipped on the light and when she saw it was Corey, she placed the gun on the counter.

"What the hell are you doing creeping around in here? You had me thinking you were a fucking intruder." She walked over and hugged him tightly.

"I wasn't creeping around. I wasn't trying to wake you up, but I see I failed. The fucking bullet almost grazed my damn ear, girl." He released her and felt his ear.

"Why? What's wrong?

She watched Corey as he took a seat on the couch and he signaled for her to sit next to him. Alyssa looked at him with wide eyes as she sat at the opposite end of the sofa and waited for him to speak.

"Look Alyssa, I know you're probably gonna want to shoot my ass for real after I tell you what I've done."

"Nigga, I'm listening." She crossed her arms over her chest.

"While I was out of town on business, I went to a party out there and ended up having a one night stand with some chick a few months back. I used a condom, but it popped while we were gettin' down. Long story short, she's pregnant and she's claimin' it's mine."

"How far along is she?"

"Almost three months." He looked at her.

"She showed me the ultrasound sound pictures and the dates do add up. When I rushed outta here, shawty was in the city and needed to see me and that's what she had to tell me."

"Do you honestly think this baby could be yours, Corey?"

"I mean…"

Alyssa slapped his ass so hard that spit flew out of his mouth before she hopped up off the sofa and dashed over to the kitchen counter where her gun was.

"Alyssa, I know you're mad, but I need you to chill the fuck out!"

"Chill the fuck out? You walked out on me a couple of weeks back because I didn't tell you about my job. You didn't talk to me for a whole week. Nigga, you just told me that you got a bitch pregnant and you got a fucking fiancée. I kept my job a secret. You've been keeping your infidelity a damn secret. This situation is bigger than that. So, don't tell me to chill the fuck out motherfucker!" She snatched her gun off the counter and walked towards him.

"Alyssa, put the fuckin' gun down. Ya ass ain't bold enough to shoot me."

"Don't fucking test me. I work for the fucking FBI. I can set this shit up and make it look like an accident and if that doesn't work, my older sister is a lawyer. So, what's it going to be?" She aimed the gun at his chest with a steady hand.

Corey bit his lip before holding his hands up to surrender. He backed away from her, picked up his bag, and found the door.

"I'm gonna give ya ass some time to cool off, but that ring better not leave ya finger. You're still mine, Alyssa."

Alyssa pulled the trigger and the bullet flew past his head and into the door.

"Next time, I won't miss."

Corey quickly opened the door and slammed it shut. She placed the gun back on the counter as she walked over to the window and watched Corey drive away. Alyssa walked into the kitchen, opened the fridge, and grabbed the half-filled pitcher of margarita. After pouring her a glass, she sat at the counter and analyzed the situation that just took place. Corey and Alyssa had been together for over a year and have been engaged for a month. Since they were in college, she always thought that he was good catch minus the fact that he was a hoe. When he wanted to make to their relationship official, Alyssa couldn't have been happier. Despite her doubtful moments of being engaged, she was always happy with Corey and couldn't have asked for a better man.

Alyssa stared down at the ring on her finger, she thought about her relationship with Corey. Chicks these days didn't leave their nigga because he cheated and a part of Alyssa wanted to be like the rest of them. It might've been easier to forgive if the possibility of a baby wasn't in the mix. She didn't know if she could raise a child that wasn't hers. Alyssa was still young and really wasn't ready to be a parent. What should have been an easy decision to make was very difficult. Alyssa wanted to be able to leave his cheating ass and move on, but it wasn't that simple. She really loved Corey and that nigga had her heart.

The bomb that Corey had dropped on her made her forget about his connection to D'Mani. Alyssa finished the pitcher and grabbed a bottle of wine from underneath the cabinet. She knew that drinking wouldn't solve her problems, but she needed to forget all her problems even if was for the moment. Between her job and loved ones, she felt like she was slowly losing her mind, but she would lose one or the other before she lost her sanity. The real question was if she had to give one up, what would it be? Her family or her career?

Chapter 17

One Week Later

As promised, Felix got back with Andrea promptly. He was one of the first people that she heard from a week ago. He gave her all of the information that he had, and at the end of the call, he made mention of another detail, but Andrea told him that if it wasn't about the man that she was looking for, then it wasn't necessary at the moment. She was sitting at home watching TV when she thought back to the first of several conversations that she had with the mystery man.

The Monday before, Andrea was at home pacing the floor as she held a piece of paper with everything that she had written down from Felix. Hannah was standing there yelling at her to make the phone call, but Andrea's nerves were getting the best of her. She felt like she had to throw up at one minute, and then the next, she wanted junk food, and the next, she was sweating and biting at her fingernails.

"Bitch... lawyer up and make the phone call!" Hannah clapped and yelled.

"I swear you make me so fuckin sick... this shit is crazy. I really had a one night stand and got pregnant by a complete fuckin stranger and you acting like this is normal!"

"Yeah yeah yeah... just make the call before I do it."

When Hannah said that, Andrea knew that it was definitely not a threat, but a promise, so she finally dialed the number.

"Hello!" the voice answered after about the fourth ring.

"Hi... umm... hello!" Andrea stuttered.

"This is awkward, but umm... I'm the... the one from Penthouse 808 and Raven Hotel."

"Oh damn... what a surprise," she could hear the smile in his voice.

"I know right." Drea relaxed a little and then continued.

"Well I know this seems stalkersih... but, I did track you down Mr. Mitchell and umm..."

"Whoaaa... let's skip all the formalities. Call me D, okay? I mean... we already explored each other and I gotta tell you, you gave a nigga some of the best sex I ever had. I wanna say the damn best, but I know how women can let that shit go to their heads," he chuckled.

Andrea couldn't help but to laugh a little, too. She finally relaxed and swatted Hannah's hands away because she kept tugging at her trying to keep her still, so that she could hear what was being said.

"Well, okay D... I can accept that since I already know your government name."

"What's yours, miss hit it and quit it?"

"Andrea, but you can call me Drea."

"Okay, Miss Drea... you ready for another round? Is that why you called?"

When he said that, reality hit again that she had to tell a total stranger that she was pregnant by him. There was no easy way to say it, so she put up a strong front and spit it out.

"I'm pregnant... I'm not asking you to do anything, but I thought letting you know would be the right thing to do... yes, it's yours because I haven't slept with anyone else and of course you can get a blood test because I'm not killing my baby."

"I see when you was dealing wit niggas in the past, they must have been some lames. Thank you for letting me know... I believe you haven't been wit anybody because that pussy was tight as fuck, like it was waiting on me. But yeah, I would love a test and yes, I will be a man and do my part. You must be a lawyer or some shit the way you went into defense mode."

"Damn... I'm sorry. This is all so crazy to me, but I actually am a lawyer," she confessed.

"I can tell," he laughed.

"That's not all," Drea whispered and the line went silent.

"I'm pregnant with twins!"

That was the first of many conversations between Andrea and D, and surprisingly she looked forward to all of his calls and texts. He checked up on her often and they discussed seeing each other soon. Andrea couldn't help, but to think about the bomb ass sex that the two of them shared and wondered if it would happen again. According to

Hannah, it was time to fuck like some dogs in heat because the damage was already done, but Andrea still couldn't help but to think about her parents. She wondered how they would react to D. For some reason, she felt like she was thirteen instead of thirty when it came to them, especially her daddy.

Andrea looked at the TV and noticed that *This Christmas* was coming on and it made her think about their dysfunctional ass family. She picked up her phone and texted her sisters in the Holiday Sisters group chat, and surprisingly her phone chimed with a reply before she could put it down.

Drea: Hey Holiday sisters! I gotta tell y'all something!

Stasia: Hey Drea! What's wrong?

Stasia: You and the baby okay?

Drea: We're fine... but, I was texting about that. Let's see if the other two gonna join us.

Lyssa: Hey y'all! What's going on?

Stasia: I'm waiting to see.

Drea: Y'all wanna do a call?

Drea: Nah never mind... but, check this out... Lexi can catch up later.

Drea: (sonogram picture)

Stasia: Omg!! You having twins?

Lyssa: TWINS???

Drea: Yes! Craziest shit EVERRR!!!

Lexi: This chat been dry as the Sahara Desert and now y'all bitches wanna light it up... let me catch up!

Stasia: This lil bitch right here... smh.

Drea: We being nice today y'all.

Lexi: You just now telling these hoes about the babies... I already knew y'all!!!!

Andrea texted Lexi on the side and cussed her out and told her to be nice.

Stasia: (rolling eyes emoji)

Lyssa: Figures you knew... but, congrats sis. Now, we gotta shop for two babies.

Stasia: Since we being nice... who's the daddy?

Lyssa: Good question.

Drea: His name is D and that's all I'm saying. Y'all will meet him soon!

Lexi: I already met him y'all!!

Lexi: J/K... LOL

Drea: Y'all coming home for Christmas?

Lexi: I ammmm...

Stasia: I really don't know, but I doubt it. It's so much going on.

Lyssa: Depends on work.

Drea: Well, I hope y'all will consider it. I know Thanksgiving wasn't the best, but we gotta start back spending as much time together as possible. Remember, we have aging parents, too.

No one replied after Drea's last text, and she really didn't expect them to. She was being sincere about them being together more and she hoped that they would put forth the effort. Since she mentioned her aging parents, she decided to get up and go visit them. Andrea knew that she had to lead by example and bury the hatchet. She had checked on them throughout the past week, but it was only by phone. The words that her mother spoke to her still rang in her head, and honestly, it all bothered her. She loved her parents dearly, but the church always came first to them and they never saw it that way.

Andrea put on her jacket and shoes and made her way next door. When she made it, the door was locked and that was strange because it was only a little after twelve, so she knew her parents should have been up. Since she didn't grab her keys, Andrea went back and got them, and then unlocked the door and let herself in. The TV wasn't on when she entered. In fact, the house was too quiet and if she didn't know any better, she would have thought that they were gone, but that wasn't possible.

"Mommm!! Daddd!!!"

She called out to them, but neither of them answered. Andrea walked to their bedroom after she left the kitchen, and the house was indeed empty. She knew they weren't upstairs, but where the hell were they? As she made her way back to the living room, the answering machine was blinking with a new message, so she hit the button and Aunt Shirley's voice and words both made her panic and become upset all at the same time.

Chapter 18

It was Saturday morning and Lexi had so much shit to do. Her last day of class was Thursday, which meant she was officially out for winter break. The thought of the New Year brought a smile to her face because she planned on doing a lot of shit different in 2018. She couldn't say that she had an awful 2017, things just took a turn for the worse the latter part of the year. Lexi was mostly excited about graduating and stepping into the real world. She had a dream last night that she landed an accounting position at Drea's law firm making crazy money. She immediately fell in love with the idea because she knew her sister had the juice to actually put her in a role like that, but that would mean she had to move back to Mississippi and that was a no go for her. She began to wonder if Alyssa could pull some strings and get her a position working as an accountant at the bureau. Living the fast life in New York fit her better than lame as Mississippi anyway. Lexi felt for her phone under the sheets; she decided to reach out to Alyssa while the idea was fresh on her brain. After searching for about fifteen seconds, she finally found her Rose Gold iPhone X and powered it on. She wondered briefly why her phone was cut off in the first place, but pushed the thought to back of her mind when she burped and tasted Patron. Lexi waited patiently for the phone to power up. Once it was on, she went to Alyssa's name in her contacts and attempted to speak to her, but it went straight to voicemail. She called right back and got the same results. Just as she was about to leave a voicemail, the loud sounds of moaning filled the air. Lexi quickly ended the call and froze momentarily as the sexual moans sounded too familiar. She turned over slowly and noticed J.R. sitting on the edge of the bed with his face buried in his phone.

"Is this nigga watching porn this early?" she said to herself before scooting over to where he was, looking over his shoulder.

"OH, MY GOOOODDD!!!" she screamed.

Lexi stared at the screen on J.R.'s phone where a video of them played from last night. Lexi rode J.R.'s dick like a professional jockey, screaming out in ecstasy.

"What the fuck? How... When.... WHAT THE FUCK J.R.!" she stuttered, admiring her skills at the same time.

"Good morning, Karrine Steffans!" J.R. stated, looking over at her briefly, and then back at his phone.

"Karrine Steffans? What the fuck you talking about?" a perplexed Lexi asked.

Instead of replying, J.R. took his finger and fast forwarded the video about two minutes ahead, showing exactly why he called her Karrine Steffans. Karrine Steffans also known as "Superhead" was famously known for her skills at sucking dick and although Lexi hated to admit it, she was giving Miss Superhead a run for her money in that video.

"Look bae, ooohhhh weeeee! You damn near got me running," J.R. laughed as he watched his reaction to the way Lexi worked her tongue on his balls.

Lexi couldn't help but laugh herself; she was doing the damn thing and deserved a pat on the back. She always enjoyed giving head, but from the performance she put on last night, it looked more like she loved doing it.

"That Henny had you acting a fool bae," J.R. stated, never taking his eyes off his phone.

"Henny? I could have sworn I had Patron," she replied, trying to collect her thoughts.

"You had both. I told you to slow down, but you told me you were grown and some mo' shit, so I shut the fuck up and let yo grown ass drink."

Lexi buried her face into the palm of her hands and sat there in silence. It seemed as if when the thought of drinking Henny and Patron hit her, so did an instant headache. The crazy thing about it all was, she never even remembered having sex, let along making a video.

"Imma need you to send me that video, and then delete the shit out yo phone," she demanded, her face still buried into her hands.

"I ain't deleting shit; I'm selling this motherfucker to Pornhub. We can get a few thousand and be straight," he replied, locking his phone, standing up, and placing it in his back pocket.

Lexi smacked her lips and laid back down on the bed. Her eyes popped open at the sound of her phone ringing. She struggled to sit up straight, but the room was spinning like she was on a carousel ride at the carnival. She let out a slight grunt, but managed to answer it before it stopped ringing.

"Hello."

"Lexi, this Tina., My flight was cancelled, you can come in now and get your nails did; I may not be back Monday in time for your appointment."

Lexi rolled her eyes so hard, you'd think that they would have gotten stuck. All she wanted to do was lay down for at least a few more hours, but she knew that Tina was always booked; it was either get her nails slayed now or walk around with her hands looking like a man.

"Ok, I'll be there in forty-five minutes," Lexi assured her before ending the call.

Forcing herself to get up, she headed into the bathroom and handled her hygiene. She took the bonnet off of her head and replaced it with a pink Clark Atlanta hat and headed out the bedroom. She grabbed a banana and a bottle of water, then told J.R. where she was headed to before hopping in her car and taking off. Tina worked in a shop almost an hour away, depending on traffic in Duluth. Lexi never minded taking the drive because she was the dopest nail tech in the Atlanta area. Bre put her on to Tina about two years ago and Lexi never allowed anyone else to touch her hands after that.

The nail shop was packed as normal when she arrived. Lexi signed in, let Tina know she was there, and waited until her name was called. She grabbed her phone out of the pocket of her jacket and paid Facebook, Snapchat, and Instagram a visit. Lexi was engrossed in her phone as she read the latest gossip in the Shade Room, a well-known Instagram page that always had the latest celebrity tea. She came across a post regarding the singer/actor, Tyrese Gibson and his latest breakdowns and shook her head. She never understood how wealthy people went through the shit that they went through, but at the end of the day, they were still humans, so she figured it was normal.

Just as Lexi was about to engage in some more ratchet fun, Tina called her name and motioned her towards her booth. Lexi stood to her feet and headed that way, but not before noticing three girls staring at her. Lexi gave them a slight mug before greeting Tina with a hug. One of the reasons Lexi loved Tina so much was because she didn't play around like most nail techs. She got you in and out regardless of how busy she was. Lexi and Tina talked about the latest bullshit going on in the world. Tina also told her about her baby daddy and how he still wasn't shit and as always, she was ready to leave him. Lexi half ass listened and she couldn't help, but notice those three girls still staring at her.

"Aye Tina, do you know them bitches that's sitting over there by the window?" Lexi asked.

Tina sat the nail filer down briefly and looked over in that direction.

"Girl, them some hood bitches from Bankhead. They don't do shit but drink, smoke weed, and cut bitches. Why?"

"They been staring at me since I walked in, but I don't know them hoes," Lexi assured her.

"Well, baby, stay clear of them. Those are some ruthless bitches, trust me when I say that."

Lexi allowed Tina's words to soak in, they soaked in so much that when Lexi went to the bathroom to wash her hands, she made sure that, not only was her taser in her purse, but that she had her mace and razor blade on her as well. After Tina put the finishing touches on Lexi's coffin nails, she prepared to leave, saying her final goodbyes to Tina, and giving her a hug.

"I knew you two wasn't going to be too far apart. Hey Bre!" Lexi heard Tina say in her ear before they released each other from their embrace.

Lexi quickly turned around, just in time to see Bre walking over towards them.

"Now, Imma have to try to fight four bitches," she said to herself, prepared for whatever was coming her way.

"Hey Tina. Hey Lexi," Bre said cheerfully before she attempted to give Lexi a hug.

"Bitch, don't touch me!" Lexi yelled, pushing Bre off of her so hard that she hit the floor.

Bre struggled to her feet laughing before charging at Lexi, but before she could make contact with her, those three girls who were staring at her earlier was dragging Bre out of the shop by her hair. Lexi along with everyone else inside, rushed outside to see the show. The three girls beat Bre's ass so bad that Lexi started to feel bad for her.

"Here come the police!" someone yelled, causing the girls to run off, leaving Bre on the ground covered in blood.

Not wanting to stay around and get questioned, Lexi too hopped in her car and peeled off. She drove 285 wondering what the fuck happened, she even more so wondered if Bre was ok. Flashbacks of those hoodlums stomping her clouded her mind as she wondered what the fuck was going on.

Buzz... Buzz... Buzz...

The sound of her vibrating phone jolted her out of her thoughts. She reached onto the passenger seat to retrieve it, but it was too late; J.R. had hung up. Lexi thought about calling him back, but figured she would just talk to him when she made it home. But, when her phone rang again and it was him, she knew that wasn't going to happen.

"Hello."

"You good?" was the first thing he asked when he heard her voice.

"Yeah, I'm good," she replied hesitantly. "Why you ask?" she continued.

"I know what just went down at the shop, Alexis," he confirmed.

"How the fuck you know?" she questioned.

"Because Diamond, Monica, and Shelly called and told me."

"And who the fuck is Shelly, Diamond, and Monica?" she questioned.

"All that don't matter, Lex…"

"Jeremy, who the fuck are those bitches?" she yelled that time, cutting him off.

"They work for me. Once you told me where you were going, I had them ride up there to check things out. To make sure you were good," he explained.

"So, you got bitches following me? I don't need no fucking babysitter," she snapped.

"First of all, watch yo mouth and secondly, if I hadn't did what I did, ain't no telling what would have happened."

"I ain't worried about no motherfucking Bre, I can handle that bitch," she hissed.

"Look baby, as long as you my girl, Imma always protect you regardless of what you say. All that hollering and shit you doing right now don't phase me. My top concern is your safety, so when you done with all that bullshit, I'll see you at home," he said, ending the call.

Lexi let out a frustrated scream while she beat the steering wheel. All she wanted to do was be great, but it was like problems followed her everywhere she went. She wanted the shit to be over, but for some reason, she felt like this was only the beginning.

Chapter 19

It had been a week since Anastasia had returned home from seeing her sister and she had successfully managed to avoid Richard despite his threats. The first day after she'd been back, she was nervous that he would show up, but by day three, she had damn near forgotten about him since he'd been so quiet. In the back of her mind, she knew that he was somewhere plotting on how to further make their divorce difficult, but she figured she would cross that bridge when she got to it.

Even not having heard from him, she took measures the entire week by getting the locks changed on her house and staying inside so that he wouldn't catch her out anywhere like he'd been doing for the last couple of weeks. She'd even went so far as to call Kyler out of school sick because she didn't want Richard to try and kidnap him from there. So, she'd been in the house all week with a busy five-year-old and she was ready to get out.

"Ma! Ma!" she was brought out of her thoughts by Kyler yelling her name and tugging on her shirt. Without turning around, she continued to apply her make-up and answered him.

"Yes Kyler?"

"Somebody at the door," he chirped and went back to sitting on her bed with his eyes glued to his tablet. Finished with her make-up, she smiled at herself in the mirror and went to answer the door.

"I'm coming!" she sang, breaking into a small run as the bell rang again. Anastasia opened the door to see Juanita standing there dressed to take on the task of a rowdy kid. She gave her a bright smile and opened the door wider.

"Hey, hun!"

"Hey, girl." Juanita walked inside taking in Anastasia's décor with a look of appreciation in her eyes. People had always admired how clean and well put-together that Anastasia kept her home; especially, with Kyler running around.

"I really appreciate you doin' this. I just.... I got cabin fever girl and I need to get out of here, even if only for a lil bit," Anastasia explained with a nervous chuckle.

"You don't have to explain nothing to me, I know what staying in the house can do, and I could use the money, so I look at it like we're helping each other," Juanita said and placed a comforting hand on her arm. Not really wanting to talk about the fact that she was out of a job because of her husband, Anastasia avoided her eyes.

"Yeah.... Uh... about that. I know that you're wondering about when I'm opening the shop back up, but trust me, I got my sister on the case and she never loses. So, it won't be long before we're back to work."

"Well, that's good to hear because I love working there," she gushed as Kyler ran into the room yelling her name.

"Ms. Nita!" In five seconds, he'd come across the room and wrapped his arms around the lady's body.

Kyler had met Juanita a few times and each time she'd managed to woo him with candy and other treats. At times, it seemed like she had a whole candy store in her purse. Anastasia watched the two interact and was happy that the situation with Richard had yet to affect him. Surprisingly, he'd only asked for his dad's whereabouts two times and had not brought it up since. She really didn't want to keep him away from his father, but the erratic behavior that Richard had been displaying lately was not something that she wanted around their son, and besides that, she didn't trust him to bring Kyler back to her. She hoped that once they straightened everything out, and got the divorce, he would return to his old stiff ass ways and simply co-parent with her.

"Kyler, go put on a movie while I show Ms. Juanita around."

"Okay! Ms. Juanita, you wanna watch the new Ninja Turtles movie?" he asked excitedly as he bounced around.

"Sure, them my boys, but Mikey is my favorite." He looked up at her in awe at the fact that she knew them by name.

"I like Mikey, too, but Leo's my favorite, and my mama likes Ralph." His small face scrunched up at that and Anastasia laughed.

"Ain't nothing wrong with Ralph, he's the bad ass."

"She always says that," Kyler explained to Juanita dryly and rolled his eyes before taking off into the living room, so that he could start the movie. Once he was out of sight Anastasia led Juanita through the house showing her where everything was and anything that she may have needed in the kitchen.

"Okay, so this should go without saying, but if Richard comes here don't let him in," she explained, looking Juanita right in the eyes.

"We're still working out the terms of the divorce, but he's made some threats that I'm not taking too lightly, and I don't want him trying to use Kyler to get to me."

"Not a problem, I can guarantee that Kyler will be safe with me," she promised before her eyes took on a sad look.

"Now, this may not be my place and I know I've only witnessed a portion of what's going on with you and your husband, but I truly hope you guys work things out so that he can see Kyler."

Anastasia didn't really know what to say to that, so she nodded and merely nodded her understanding. She took it with a grain of salt because no one truly knew the things that she was going through with Richard, and in that sense, could not comment on anything she was doing to protect herself and her son in this situation.

After she finished getting herself together, she was out of the door in the next fifteen minutes and on her way to her sister's house. When she pulled up, she sent Alyssa a quick text to let her know that she was outside. It didn't take her long to come out and jump in the car with a smile.

"Hey sister!" she gushed, giving her a hug.

"Hey boo! I see you lookin all cute," Anastasia complimented. She was happy to see her sister again and ready to spill the tea on all of the things that had been going on since they hadn't spoken in a while.

"Let me find out Corey over here putting in that good work." She laughed and was surprised that Lyssa didn't join her.

"I'd rather not talk about him right now," she quipped and cast her eyes towards the window. Anastasia wanted to ask her about was going on, but she didn't want to upset her sister and figured that if she wanted to talk about it, she would. She decided she would just let her off with some advice, and then leave it alone.

"Okay well, whatever it is, I'm sure you guys can work it out. But, if you feel like it's not fixable, then don't hesitate to leave that nigga in the dust. The last thing I want is for you to end up in an unhappy relationship or marriage because it looks good." Anastasia knew that her sister was aware she was talking about herself and her situation, but due to them not having talked, she didn't know about the new shit Richard had done.

"I know, I know, but what's going on with you?"

Anastasia sighed and pulled out of the driveway before filling her sister in on the last couple of weeks. She told her everything from the beginning with Richard, starting from the day they had returned from Thanksgiving. Of course, Alyssa sat and gasped at almost everything that she said; especially, when she got to the part about her going to see Drea. By the time she finished, they were at the mall and Alyssa's mouth had dropped like ten times.

"Bitch, I'm ready to go plant some evidence on that nigga!" she fumed as they exited the car and began to walk into the mall doors. Anastasia couldn't help but laugh at her sister for even saying that shit out loud. The crazy part was that she believed that she would do it for real.

"While you over there laughing, I'm dead ass serious."

"I know fool, but what type of sister would I be to let you do something that would jeopardize your career? Besides, Richard's bitch ass ain't even worth it."

"Jeopardize? Who said I'ma get caught, bitch? It ain't nothin to go in that evidence room and get to pullin out lil bags of coke for his ass. Then, I'd just make an anonymous tip, and tah dah! One less nigga you gotta worry about." She shrugged as if it were really that simple.

"Girl, yo ass crazy!" Anastasia chuckled, pulling her sister into Nordstrom and going straight to their bags.

"I ain't too crazy." She rolled her eyes and admired the purses alongside her sister before continuing.

"But, um…. you haven't mentioned your side boo in a while…. wassup with him?"

Anastasia noticed the little slick way that her sister tried to ease D'Mani into the conversation, but there wasn't really anything to tell. She tilted her head to the side as she continued to browse and shrugged.

"There's nothing to mention. We haven't really talked much since before Thanksgiving, and real talk, I got too much shit going on to even be thinking about his ass right now."

The truth was that she had been avoiding D'Mani's calls since she saw him at his house with that other woman. As bad as she wanted to talk to him, she just wasn't ready to deal with him right now. She couldn't deny that she was no doubt hurt about the way that he acted that day, and the fact that it took him a full 24 hours before he actually tried to call her. Alyssa gave her a funny look and smacked her lips.

"So, since y'all "broke up"?" she asked using air quotes.

"Do that mean that you gone finally tell me who he is?"

"Nope," Anastasia said simply and moved on to another rack. There was no way that she was ever going to disclose D'Mani's identity; especially, since she wasn't planning on there being a future for them. Alyssa followed her and began looking through the racks with her, but she caught the hint and dropped the subject.

"Sooooo, how was the trip out there with Drea?" She wanted to know, sparking up another conversation.

"It actually wasn't that bad," Stasia told her, happy that she took heed to the fact that she wasn't on the D'Mani topic.

"We both were surprisingly on our best behavior, but let me tell you bout yo drunk ass Aunty, girl."

"Aww shit! What Aunt Shirley was on?"

"Why did we run into Zyree?"

"Zyree?" Lyssa interrupted with a frown.

"Yes, bitch, Zyree! He wasn't talkin' bout shit, but Shirley ass saw him and tried to say Kyler might be his son!"

"Well, I wasn't gone say nothin' buuuut, he do kinda look like dude." Lyssa looked as if the resemblance between the two should have been obvious.

"No, the hell he don't," Anastasia argued and waved her sister off.

"You and Aunty Shirley ready to start some shit over nothin. There is no way that Kyler is Zyree's baby." She quickly dismissed the idea. The last thing Anastasia needed was the added drama from Zyree thinking he was Kyler's father. She rolled her eyes as Alyssa mumbled a "whatever" under her breath.

"Don't be whatevering me, hoe. Come on let's go and eat cause you rude when you hungry."

They both laughed knowing that what she'd said was the truth. Alyssa ass always acted up when she was hungry and if she didn't get something in her soon, her attitude was only going to get worse.

"Fuck you, but come on cause I am hungry," she managed to say as she threw the shirt she was looking at on the top of the other clothes.

They decided to just grab a bite from the food court, so that they wouldn't have to travel far. They rode the escalator down to get there. Alyssa wanted pizza and Stasia was craving some fries from Burger King, so they separated just long enough to get their food and then met back at a table. Of course, the conversation flowed much better once Alyssa's ass had some food in her. They laughed and joked about some of everything under the sun as they ate, and once they were finished, Anastasia realized that she had to go to the bathroom. After dumping their trays, they both walked over to the bathroom and entered a stall. Somehow Anastasia finished first and as she approached the sink, Lizz walked in and locked eyes with her in the mirror. She immediately froze and stood up straight.

"Hey Lizz," Anastasia chirped with a smile. She knew the day would come when she would catch that hoe;

she just never figured that it would be so soon. The look on her face alone was enough to make Anastasia chuckle.

"Don't look scared now, bitch."

"Oh, I'm not scared…surprised maybe. I figured you wouldn't be ready to show your face outside." She let out a fake giggle, but stopped when she heard the toilet flush indicating that they weren't alone. Alyssa stepped out of the stall and fear flashed across her face knowing she was out numbered.

"Oh, you ain't got shit to say now, huh?" Alyssa taunted her and stepped in between the two so that she could wash her hands.

"Fuck you waiting for Stasia, beat this hoe ass," she told her sister in the mirror and as if a switch had been flipped, Anastasia pounced on Lizz, punching her right in the nose. She continued to pummel her fist into Lizz's face while she moaned and screamed loudly.

"Bitch, shut yo ass up! You wasn't cryin' when you was fuckin' my sister man!" Alyssa shouted joining in the fight and adding a couple of swings and a couple of kicks, before pulling her sister off of the bloody hoe. She bent down and pulled her badge out of her purse and put it in Lizz's face as she whimpered quietly.

"You see this, bitch? I'm the police, so if you even think about pressin' charges, I'm gone come fuck you up way worse, and then put yo ass in jail! Don't play with me!" she mushed her in the face, and then stepped around her body to leave.

Before leaving, Anastasia snatched up Lizz's purse and opened her wallet, pulling out the black card that bared Richard's name. "I'll take this, thank you," she said flipping her hair. She dropped her purse on the floor next to her and followed her sister out of the bathroom.

"Stasia, did you rob that bitch?" Lyssa asked laughing as they hurried out of the mall and to her car.

"Lyssa, did you threaten to arrest and beat her?"

"Hell yeah!" they both said in unison as they reached Anastasia's car and hopped inside. For some reason, Stasia couldn't wait to let her other sisters know about them finally catching Lizz. The day had definitely turned out to be a good one.

Chapter 20

Work was the only thing on Alyssa's mind since she slapped the taste out of Corey's mouth. Corey blew her phone up with calls and texts and the gifts were never ending. The jewelry, designer bags, shoes and clothes were to die for and if she was the type of bitch whose pussy got wet whenever a nigga showered her with designer things, Alyssa would've forgave Corey in a heartbeat. When she wasn't focused on the case, she spent most her time thinking about his one nightstand that could possibly be his baby mama. The love she had for Corey was strong, but she'd be damned if she was going to be anyone's fool.

Although there was a little tension between the two, Alyssa was glad when she met up with Anastasia for lunch. Alyssa had been worried about her sisters' well-being since they returned home and for Anastasia to not return her calls or send her text, pissed her off more than anything. Alyssa understood that Anastasia was going through a lot with the divorce and after she got finished telling her about the bullshit he was putting her through, Alyssa was ready to kill Richard's lame ass. The anger that Alyssa had inside of her was unleashed when they saw Lizz at the restaurant. That ass whooping was long overdue and that bitch deserved every lick she received.

Alyssa and Tara became the dynamic duo as they continued to make progress on their case. They continued to take photos of the flirt from the club and the chick that did the drop offs, which kept leading them to different locations and more useful evidence. Tara would come by her house every other day with new photos and information about their target, but Alyssa felt that there was something else going on. When Tara would look at the photos that Alyssa took of the flirt from the club and D'Mani, Tara's demeanor would change from happy to angry almost instantly. She never asked her partner any questions about the man in the picture. Alyssa figured that the truth would come out sooner or later or Tara would tell her when she was ready.

Alyssa was awakened by a call from the chief. He called her that morning telling her to meet him in his office immediately and the tone in his voice made her uneasy. Taking a quick shower, she got dressed in a simple white button up shirt, black pants and a pair of ankle boots. She snatched her rollers out of her hair, grabbed her purse and coat before jogging out the door. Alyssa weaved in and out of traffic and when she arrived at headquarters, she came to a screeching halt as she pulled into the nearest parking spot. After jogging up the steps, she swiped her badge before entering the building, making a beeline towards the elevator. When she reached her floor, Alyssa took a moment to catch her breath. She opened the double doors and as she made her way to the chief's office, she noticed that one of her team members was looking at her with a smirk on his face. She was confused as to why he was smirking at her, but she brushed it off.

The chief's door was open when she approached, but she knocked before she walked in.

"Good morning, Ms. Holiday. Close the door and take a seat." Chief Griffin pointed to the chair in front of his desk.

Closing the door, Alyssa sat in the chair and waited for him to speak.

"Ms. Holiday, since joining the FBI, you've been doing well as an agent. I admire your work ethic, take charge attitude, and how you seem to be putting forth more effort than the veterans on the team."

"Thank you, sir," she beamed.

"Don't thank me just yet. It has been brought to my attention that you have been withholding information as well as evidence from this team which has caused me to question your involvement with this case," he stated with a serious tone.

"Excuse me?"

Chief Griffin pushed an envelope across the desk and motioned for her to open it. Alyssa pulled out the pictures and slowly looked through them. As she studied the pictures, she realized that the pictures in her hand were the same pictures on her camera. There were a few pictures of her walking into the club and her leaving. She bit the inside of her jaw before she placed the photos back in the envelope. Somebody was trying to set her up.

"Can you explain to me why you haven't presented these to the team or to me?"

"Chief Griffin, I didn't tell you about the pictures because I wanted to be the one to take down D'Mani Mitchell. I have no ties to the target or anyone in his organization," she expressed with sincerity.

"What about the photos of you entering and exiting the club?"

"I was there undercover, sir. The owner of one of those vehicles owns that club and while I was there, I found out that our target is the co-owner. They're probably using the club as a front. Believe me when I tell you, sir, my only involvement in this case is to help bring the target in."

"Do you know how useful this information is? We probably would've caught him by now if you would've given me this information at an earlier date, Ms. Holiday. I want to believe that you're here for the right reason, but what you just revealed to me heightens my suspicions of your involvement with Mr. Mitchell. As of right now, you are under investigation and suspended until further notice.

"Chief Griffin, please don't--."

"Good day, Ms. Holiday!" he roared.

Feeling defeated, Alyssa got up to leave.

"Oh, and Ms. Holiday? You should be mindful of how you handle yourself outside of work. FBI agents shouldn't fight in public."

The mention of the fight caused Alyssa to lock eyes with the chief once more before walking out the office. She grabbed a few empty boxes and cleaned off her desk. The members of her he team questioned her about what happened, but she didn't tell them much. She just told them that she was suspended until further notice. Most of them seemed sincerely sad to hear the news, but the one that didn't ask any questions was the co-worker that was smirking at her when she entered. He mostly kept to himself, so the fact that he didn't ask any questions didn't bother her at all.

When Alyssa went to empty out the last drawer, she noticed that the drawer had been broken into. Alyssa rushed out the office a couple of days ago and left her camera on her desk. She called Tara and told her to lock it up in her desk drawer. When she went to get it, it was still there, but she didn't realize that the latch was broken. She quickly put the pieces together and realized that someone made copies of her photos and added a few of their own. Alyssa thought about who would want to set her up and the only person that came to mind was Tara.

She put the last of her things in the boxes and marched out of headquarters. As Alyssa made her way to the parking lot, she saw Tara coming in.

"Hey Alyssa. Why do you have those boxes?"

"Thanks to you, I got suspended."

"What? How did I get you suspended?" she asked with confusion.

"I know you had some shit going on with you, but I never would've thought that you would stab me in the back like this. I guess you wanted me out of the way so you take all the credit for yourself huh?" Alyssa expressed with anger.

"Alyssa, what are you talking about?"

"Somebody broke into my drawer and made copies of the pictures on my camera and turned them into the chief. He thinks I'm a part of D'Mani's organization and now, I'm under investigation and suspended until further notice."

"What? Wait! You think I did that?!" she asked in shock.

Alyssa just stared at her.

"Alyssa, I consider you a friend and I wouldn't stab you in the back like that. I locked your camera up like you told me to. I swear," she raised her right hand.

Alyssa didn't respond, she just walked off and left Tara standing there. She popped the trunk, placed her things inside, and jumped behind the wheel. She pulled out of the parking lot and drove home. When she arrived home, she got her things out of her trunk and carried them inside the Condo. Alyssa sat the boxes down in her bedroom and let out a sigh of frustration. As she thought about the conversation she had with Tara, she felt like she made a mistake in accusing her of getting her suspended. Alyssa never had any doubts about her before, but being as though she had the most info on her at the moment, that was her first guess. With no job and the fact the she still wasn't talking to Corey, she didn't know what she was going to do for the upcoming holiday. She thought about the group chat with her sisters and how Andrea said that they should think about coming home for Christmas. Without hesitation, she hopped up and started packing her bags.

Chapter 21

Andrea couldn't believe what she heard. Aunt Shirley was loud and crazy, but she wasn't one to make up shit and it definitely wouldn't benefit her to make up a lie about her dad being in the hospital. Andrea stood there in shock as she replayed the message and processed it.

"I just got your last message sister, I'm on my way. I'll meet you at UMC... lawd I can't stand Abraham 'ol coon ass, but I don't want him to die on you!"

She didn't know if she was more hurt or angry that her mom really didn't call or come next door to let her know that her dad was going to the hospital. She loved her parents despite all of the drama that was going on and she assumed as Christians and as her parents, they would have put their differences to the side by now and tried to move forward. Andrea went back home and locked up, and then headed towards the University of Medical Center, where she heard Aunt Shirley mention on the answering machine.

Andrea hopped in her car and fought back tears at the thought of losing her dad. She was going to be the bigger person and not bring up the pettiness when she arrived, but she had to vent to someone, so she called her best friend.

"Heeyyy... is that fine man here yet? Oh wait, that's next weekend. I'm getting ahead of myself!" Hannah exclaimed.

"Hannah... why is my daddy in the hospital and I had to find out by hearing Aunt Shirley on the answering machine when I went next door to check on them?"

"Whaaatttt? Your parents taking this whole pregnancy thing to a different level. Don't the bible say you supposed to forgive and shit?"

"Exactly! I don't care what I did… I'm not apologizing in front of a church. For what?"

"I don't blame you… well you gotta stop stressing. You got two other people to think about. How serious is it with your dad?"

"I really don't know. I'm on my way to find out. I need to call my sister's, but I kinda wanna see how serious everything is before I alarm them."

"Yeah, that's probably a good idea since none of them are in Mississippi. I'll meet you there. What hospital?"

"UMC."

Andrea hung up with her friend and continued to the hospital. An eerie feeling came over her and she couldn't shake it. As she drove down Lakeland, she began looking in her rearview mirror constantly because it seemed like she was being followed. She turned the music on in hopes that it would erase her thoughts and feelings, but even with a gospel song playing, it did no good. It was Saturday evening, so traffic was crazy. After twenty minutes of riding on Lakeland alone, Drea finally turned onto State Street. She had to quickly decide whether or not she was going to park in parking garage A or B. From past experiences, A was always full, so she opted for B. After getting a ticket from the dispenser, she put it in her windshield and drove from level to level in search of the first available space.

She finally found one on level three and it was close to the elevator, so it was perfect. Drea parked, grabbed her phone and purse, and hoped out. Out of nowhere, a car sped towards her and if she had not jumped back, she would have been laid out on the concrete. Her heart rate increased rapidly.

"Ma'am… are you okay?" a lady practically ran up and panicked.

"Ye… yeah… just a little shaken up."

"Looks like that person tried to hit you. They had a hat pulled down over their face, so I couldn't see if it was a man or woman."

She knew that whoever it was, it had to be whomever was following her. Drea felt like it wasn't a coincidence, but she had no idea who would be after her and for what. After checking her surroundings again and thanking the kind woman for checking on her, Andrea made her way to the hospital. She walked to the receptionist and asked for Abraham Holiday's room number. Andrea gasped when she was told that he was in the critical care unit on the third floor and hurriedly made her way to the elevator. Even though her parents and even aunt had cell phones, they never used them, so it wouldn't do her any good to call them.

Andrea was glad to be on the elevator alone because she was sure that she looked how she felt, which was a total mess. She got off the elevator when it chimed and read the numbers on the wall so that she could go in the right direction. She heard her aunt's mouth coming from the opposite direction that she was about to go, so Drea turned around and headed that way. A waiting room sign was ahead, so she was sure that was where her voice was coming from.

"Now Vicky, you know you wrong... you hiding shit from your kids like that. God ain't pleased and yo ass should know that before me," Aunt Shirley fussed.

Andrea heard her mom huff, but she never replied. Deciding not to waste any time, she walked in and made her presence known. She locked eyes with her mom and there was nothing, but tension in the room.

"Oh shit! Vicky y'all done pissed these kids off and now they fed up!" Aunt Shirley expressed.

"How's dad?" Drea asked instead of saying what was really on her mind.

"He's fine... how did you know we were up here?"

"I don't think it really matters mom. Why didn't you tell me though?" she couldn't hold it in any longer.

"It's not the time nor the place, Andrea!" her mom scolded.

"Well, when is the time and place?" Aunt Shirley chimed in.

"Shirley... stop the nonsense!"

"Don't get mad at me... humph. You know I'm right!"

"What's going on with dad and how long have y'all been here?" Drea quizzed.

"They are running some tests on his heart, but he's fine," her mom answered the first part of the question, but then skipped the second one.

"Where is he? I'm going to see him!"

"It's not visitation time yet," her mom stated.

Andrea rolled her eyes and walked away. With the way that she was feeling, there was no telling what was going to come out of her mouth, so she left to keep from disrespecting her mother. Before she made it down the hall, she heard Aunt Shirley calling out to her. Drea slowed her pace and let her aunt catch up.

"Damn... slow down... You tryna give me a heart attack like..." she started saying, but cut her sentence short.

When she cut her sentence short, Drea knew that something was terribly wrong because Aunt Shirley didn't give a damn what she said or did.

"What's going on Aunt Shirley?"

"Your mom is just upset and thinks keeping the information from you girls is the right thing to do, but it ain't. Now, I'm not supposed to tell you, but you might wanna tell your sisters that their daddy is very sick. He gotta have triple bypass surgery, but they can't do it until he gets stronger and that might take a few days."

Tears streamed down Drea's face as she listened to her aunt. All of the anger that she had felt was gone and had been replaced by nothing, but hurt. She needed her daddy to be okay. Instead of replying to Aunt Shirley, she fell into her arms and cried. Her aunt comforted her and they walked downstairs to get some fresh air. The next visitation was scheduled for five o'clock. They didn't have long to wait. Drea decided to go ahead and text the Holiday sisters to let them know that their dad was in the hospital.

Chapter 22

Right after the nail shop incident, Lexi went straight to the crib and cursed J.R. out. She had rehearsed the entire argument in the car and to her surprise, when she got face to face with him, everything went as planned. J.R. tried to explain himself and defend his actions, but regardless of how he put things, Lexi wasn't having it. Alexis noticed that J.R. was big on protection, which made her nervous altogether. She wondered was her life in danger just because she was his girl; if so, she needed to reevaluate the whole relationship shit. When she dreamed about being with thugs, she meant the niggaz in the Urban Fiction books she read, not no real pistol toting ass nigga like the one she had.

"You know what Jeremy, I'm tired of arguing with you." She finally said, after going back and forth for what seemed like an hour.

"You should have been tired cuz ain't shit gon change ALEXIS......You kill me saying a motherfucker Government name like it mean sum," he said, chuckling lightly before walking out of the room.

Lexi got up and headed to where her purse was located, which was over on the chaise not too far from the closet. She had made a stop at Walgreens and got some Nyquil because her throat had been feeling itchy all day and she wanted to catch the cold before it ruined her life. She grabbed her bottle of water that was on the nightstand and knocked it back with two pills in the mixture. She then got up and showered before the medicine kicked it. After she washed her ass, she headed back to bed just in time because she was starting to feel sleepy. Lexi played a game she downloaded on her phone called, *Home Design,* until she couldn't play no more. Just as she began to dose off,

Marcus called twice. She ignored both calls, and then put her phone on "Do Not Disturb" and finally drifted off to sleep land.

The next morning, Lexi woke up from the best rest she'd had in a long time. Not only had her throat stopped hurting, she felt rejuvenated. She turned over onto her side and noticed that J.R. was not lying next to her. She immediately got up, headed to the bathroom to empty her bladder and brush her teeth, before heading downstairs to see if he was still in the house. She didn't have to look far, she found him laid across the couch with the remote in his hands, watching NBA highlights.

"Hey baby!" she said, greeting him with a smile, jumping off the last step.

"Don't hey baby me. Bruh, we still into it," he replied sitting up.

"But, I don't wanna be into it anymore," she whined, poking her bottom lip out while joining him on the couch.

J.R. shook his head laughing before pulling her into a playful head lock.

"I'm glad you woke, I gotta talk to you about something," J.R. said, releasing his grip and cutting off the TV.

For a moment, Lexi got nervous. Usually when niggaz got that serious, they either had a secret wife or a shorty on the way, either way, Lexi wasn't there for none of it. She sat next to him waiting patiently for him to spill the beans.

"Imma have to go to New York next month to handle some business," he stated.

"Ok, everything good?" she wondered.

"Yeah everything straight, it's just that, I may be gone for about two months…"

"TWO MONTHS! WHAT THE FUCK YOU GON BE DOING IN NEW YORK FOR TWO MONTHS?"

"Look, chill…. I gotta handle some business. Seeing how you still gon be in school, I'll get you a flight every weekend just so yo lil ass won't go crazy," he explained.

Lexi felt a little better knowing that she wasn't going two months straight without seeing him, but she still was hurt that he was leaving her.

"What kind of business?" she questioned.

"The kind of business I DO! I keep telling you that the less you know, the better," he replied.

Lexi hated when he told her that shit, but she knew she had to respect it. She knew niggaz like J.R. and she knew that you had to earn their loyalty and trust and she chose to follow his lead because she was really into him.

"So, when you leaving?"

"I don't know the exact date yet, but when I find out, I'll let you know," he assured her.

"Yup!" was all she said before standing up and heading back upstairs.

"What the fuck wrong with you now?" he yelled out to her.

"Shit! I'm going upstairs to call my mom, if that's ok with you," she smirked, leaving him sitting on the couch alone.

Once back inside the bedroom, she grabbed her phone, noticing a bunch of missed calls and unread messages. The calls were mainly from Marcus and a few other friends. After scrolling through the call log, she went and read the text messages, starting with the one from her mom.

Mommy: Good morning baby, I'm at the hospital with dad so if you call, I most likely won't have service. I'll call you when I leave. Love you!

Lexi's heart started beating rapidly. She wondered why her father was back in the hospital, she knew it had to be serious because it was Sunday and Abraham's leg could be falling off and his ass would still limp into that church. Instead of texting her mother back, she called three times in a row and got the voicemail. She then pulled up the text message that she got from Drea and her heart fell into her stomach.

Drea: I texted the group message, but I know yo ass never read our shit, but daddy is back in the hospital. I'm not sure how serious it is, but I'm worried.

After reading that message, Lexi tossed her phone on the bed and headed to the closet to grab her Louie Vuitton duffle bag. She began to stuff panties, bras, and other little knickknacks inside. She then went inside the closet and grab whatever she could fold, tossing it in the duffle bag as well.

"Where the fuck you going?" J.R. asked entering the room.

"Home!"

"Home? Really Lexi, you doing all this extra shit because of the bullshit at the nail shop and the fact I gotta go take care of some business? You leaving me shorty?" he asked in a serious tone followed by a light chuckle.

Lexi stopped what she was doing and stared at him. For the first time since they've been together, she seen worry in his eyes. That worry made butterflies form in her stomach because she knew that he really cared about her.

"My father is really sick, both my sister and mom texted me this morning and told me," she replied, trying to hold back tears.

Before she could start back packing, J.R. pulled her into his arms where she allowed the first tear to fall. The uncertainty was killing her and deep down in her heart, she felt like something serious was going on with her dad.

"I'm about to see if we can get a flight out," J.R. said, releasing her and grabbing his phone.

"Imma just drive, it's only five hours away," she replied, heading into the bathroom to get her feminine hygiene products.

"Cool, we can take my truck, I need to put some miles on the bitch anyway."

Lexi watched J.R. move around the room, throwing shit inside his MCM duffle bag. A smile crept across her face as she watched her man come to her aid. Lexi always wondered how her family would react when they first met him, and it was time to see.

Lexi and J.R. hit the road after grabbing a to-go meal from Denny's. They gassed up his G-Wagon and headed 20-West towards Mississippi. Lexi sat in the passenger seat comfortable wearing a jogging suit she got from Victoria Secret Pink. She tossed off her Uggs, reclined her seat back, and enjoyed the ride. Her mind was still on her father's health, so she tried calling her mother again a dozen times, still with no success.

"It's crazy that it takes near death experiences to happen for people to realize the joy of life," Lexi said out the blue as she stared at the traffic in front of her.

"Yeah, that's usually how life works. I never said anything to you before about this, but you and your sisters need to make amends. Y'all parents are aging and y'all all y'all got," J.R. replied, looking over at her briefly, and then back at the road.

Lexi allowed his words to sink in. Regardless of the differences her and her sisters have, once their parents are gone, they would only have each other.

"You know what baby, you right. I got an idea., Lexi said, pulling her phone and credit card out her purse.

J.R. turned a five-hour drive into four hours and Lexi couldn't have been happier. She was tired of sitting in the car and on top of that, her nerves were getting the best of her. Lexi gave J.R. turn by turn directions as they made their way to her parents' house. When they pulled up, she noticed her father's car was there, but her mother's truck wasn't, which meant that her mother was still at the hospital. She had him park behind her father's ride, but when they got out, she headed across the lawn to Drea's house.

"I thought you said your parents stay right here." J.R. said, pointing to the house she grew up in.

"Yeah, but my sister Drea lives next door and I can see that she's home," she explained to him as she walked across the manicure lawn.

Lexi went to the door and rang the doorbell, seconds later Drea's voice could be heard from the other side asking, "Who is it?". Lexi purposely stayed silent while Drea asked two more times. Seconds later, an angry Drea snatched the door open, clearly ready to go off on the visitor standing on the other side, but when she noticed her little sister standing there, a huge smile invaded her face.

"Babbbyyy Holiday! What are you doing here?" she asked, greeting her sister with a big hug.

"I came as soon as I got your text message. I've been calling mommy, but her phone is powered off," Lexi replied, pulling away from her sister and rubbing her harden belly.

"Awwww my TT Babies in there. Heyyyy y'all, this is your favorite auntie, Sexy Lexi," Lexi bent down and spoke into Drea's belly.

"Girl stop! You so stupid…. Stupid and rude," Drea said pushing Lexi to the side while smiling at J.R.

"Hey, I'm Andrea and I take it you're J.R," She continued, extending her arm for a handshake, but he left her hanging.

"J.R.? Who is J.R.?" he asked looking between Lexi and Drea.

"Oh shit, I'm sorry," Drea apologized, her face turning red.

"Nah, I'm bullshitting. How you doing, ma?" J.R. replied, pulling Drea into a hug while Lexi bent over in laughter.

"Oh, my God! Why you do me like that? Y'all two belong together. Bring y'all ass in here," Drea replied, moving out the way, allowing them to come in.

Once inside, Drea offered both Lexi and J.R. something to eat and drink, but they both declined. Drea also ran down everything that happened from the time she heard the message up until the conversation with Aunt Shirley in the hallway. Lexi told her that she was going to stop by the hospital once they checked in at the hotel, but Drea insisted that the two of them stayed there, which shocked the shit out of Lexi. After confirming that J.R. was cool with it, she gave in to her sister demands and planned on crashing in her guest room.

"Have you talked to Anastasia or Alyssa?" Drea asked Lexi.

"Nope, but I'm hoping they making plans to come here because..."

BOOM...

A loud bang came from upstairs, which caused everyone in the living room to freeze.

"What the fuck was that?" Lexi looked at Drea and asked.

"Aw girl, I forgot her ass was up there sleep," she replied.

"Who?" Lexi questioned.

"MEEEEEEEEEEEE!!" Aunt Shirley yelled, walking down the stairs.

Lexi buried her face inside the palms of her hands and shook her head. Aunt Shirley came prancing in the living room wearing a pink floral sweater, green corduroy pants, and some pink Sketchers.

"Hey Auntie," Lexi spoke, lifting her head up.

"Heyyyy girl! What you doing here?" she asked.

"I came to check on my dad," Lexi answered her.

"Mmmmmmphhhh... Anyway, who is this?" Shirley asked, staring at J.R.

"This my boyfriend, J.R."

"Boyfriend? Thank you, Jesus! Lexi, I thought you was gon' be bumping coochies ya whole life," Shirley blurted out causing J.R. and Drea to laugh.

"Nah Auntie, I made her forget about bumping coochies." J.R. bragged while looking over at Lexi and licking his lips.

"I bet you did with yo fine ass. Now, do what it takes to make me forget, too," Shirley said, winking her eye at him.

Lexi laughed before standing up and grabbing J.R.'s hand, "Auntie I'll fight you over this one," Lexi promised her.

"And you'll lose every time," Aunt Shirley replied, before smacking J.R. on the ass as they made their exit, heading towards the guest room.

Chapter 23

Alyssa gazed out the window of the plane as she twiddled her thumbs. She had been anxious to get back home since she received the text from Andrea, Saturday evening about their father being in the hospital. She wanted to fly out Sunday evening, but she didn't like the flight time, but she found a flight for early Monday morning and arrived at the airport an hour before her flight. With her father being in the hospital and her suspension, Alyssa was in a state of depression. She hoped she could put on a strong front for her family, but even if she couldn't, that would be okay with her. Alyssa's mind was filled with how she acted towards her family over the years and how the distance put a strain on her relationship with her parents. The fiasco at church played heavily in her head and she couldn't help, but to feel like she was responsible for her father being in the hospital yet again.

When her plane touched down in Mississippi, she grabbed her carry-on and exited the plane. Alyssa power walked towards the airport exit and stole a cab from a couple that was about to get in. Slamming the door shut and locking it, she tossed a couple of hundreds at the driver and gave him the address to the University of Mississippi Medical Center. Alyssa reached in her backpack and grabbed her cell, powering it on. She had a few texts messages, missed calls, and voicemails from Corey and before she could read his texts, an incoming call from him came through.

"Yes Corey?" she answered annoyed.

"Why the fuck I get to ya crib to make up with ya ass and you ain't the fuck here?" his voice boomed through the phone.

"Last time I checked, I was grown and I didn't think I needed to inform anybody about the moves I made," she snapped back.

"Kill the fuckin' attitude for a minute and just talk to me. Just because you mad at nigga don't mean you stopped lovin' me. I'm still ya nigga and you're still my wife. So, what the fuck is up?"

Alyssa let out a sigh of frustration before she answered.

"I got a text from Drea on Saturday about our father being in the hospital. I just touched down in Mississippi not too long ago and I'm on my way to the hospital now."

"What the hell is goin' on with ya pops?"

"I don't know. She just said the he was in the hospital and I came running. If it's anything serious, I'll let you know."

"Aight, but I'll be there by the end of the week though."

"For what, Corey?" she asked confused.

"Because you need me there, Alyssa. I'm not gonna let this feud keep me away from you when you're goin' through a tough time. I'll check in with you later, aight?"

"Okay."

"I love you."

She remained silent.

"I said I love you, Alyssa," he spoke a little louder.

"I love you too, Corey."

The call ended and she kept her phone in her hand as she gazed out the window. Alyssa couldn't help the smile that appeared on her face as she thought about Corey and the conversation they just had. His fuck up still didn't sit right with her, but the way he never left her alone since he confessed his sins to her made her feel as if she was still his number one choice. Even though she didn't know what he was doing in his spare time, it never stopped him from texting her and telling her how much he missed her, loved her, and how sorry he was. Corey was trying to break her down and she hated to admit it, but his efforts were working.

The driver pulled up to the hospital a little while later and Alyssa told the driver to keep the meter running before she hopped out. She walked up to the nurses' station and asked for her father and when the nurse told her that her father was in critical care, she began to panic. After she thanked the nurse, she walked quickly towards the elevator, hopping on before the door closed. She stepped off when she reached her floor and headed straight for her father's room. Alyssa walked in his room letting the door close behind her. When he turned his head towards her, she smiled.

"Hey Dad." She grabbed his hand when she reached his bed side.

"Hey sweetheart. What a surprise." He sat up in bed.

"I know you weren't expecting to see me, but I had to come and check on you." She gave a small smile.

"I'm glad you came."

"So, what's going on with you?"

208

"Well, I'm having surgery when I get strong enough to handle it."

"What kind of surgery?"

"Triple bypass."

"What?"

"Alyssa, calm down."

"I can't calm down, dad. When I called mom a couple of weeks ago, she said you were okay. How did you being okay turn into you needing triple bypass surgery?" She fought back tears.

"Why am I just finding out about this? Did Andrea know all this time and not tell me?"

"No, she found out when you did." Victoria entered the room.

"I didn't tell you or your sisters about what your father because I felt like y'all didn't need to know. Especially you."

"What do you mean, mom? This is our father we're talking about and his health is important to us, even if you don't feel as though it is." She tried to hold back her anger but couldn't.

"Why would I tell you anything, Alyssa?"

"Victoria, please," her father chimed in.

"You're the one responsible for putting him here. He wouldn't need to have surgery if it wasn't for you," venom laced her voice as she spoke.

Her mother's words hit her like a ton of bricks.

"He was fine until you told him that you were an FBI agent and was determined not to quit. Add that to the spiteful act against your sister at church, you almost killed your father. Are you back to finish the job?" her mother shouted.

Alyssa wanted to cry, but she wouldn't give her mother the satisfaction of seeing her tears.

"Dad, I'll be home for a while. So, if you need anything just call me, okay?"

"I will, Alyssa."

"Mom, I guess I'll see you at home. I love y'all."

Abraham was the only one who said I love you back as she walked out the door. She took the stairs instead of the elevator and jogged out of the hospital and to the cab. Alyssa jumped inside and gave the driver the address to her parents' house. Not being able to hold her tears back any longer, she let them fall. As she approached her childhood home, she tossed an extra hundred to the driver before grabbing her suitcase and exiting the cab. Alyssa walked up the porch steps and into the house. She knew right away that Aunt Shirley was there. The smell of alcohol mixed with whatever she was cooking, hit her nose.

"Who the hell is that out there?" her aunt yelled from the kitchen.

"It's Alyssa, Aunt Shirley." she announced when she entered.

"Well look who dropped in. I thought ya ass woulda been the last one to pop in to see about your dad."

"Did you see him yet?"

"Yeah I just came from the hospital. I was actually happy about seeing him until my mom blamed me for putting him in there." Alyssa flopped down in the chair.

"She did what?" she turned around to face her.

"Yeah. She blames me for everything. She even asked me if I came back to finish the job."

"That damn girl," her aunt huffed.

"You, your sisters, and all y'all damn secrets did a number on your parents, but I don't agree with her shuttin' y'all out and not tellin' y'all what was goin' on with Abraham. I've been tryin' to explain to her that children have to grow up and live their own lives, and instead of bein' mad at the decisions y'all make, they need to be more supportive."

"It doesn't matter now, Aunt Shirley. My father is laying up in the hospital because of me and now, he needs to have surgery. This is all my fault." She began to cry again.

"Ain't no time to be throwin' a damn pity party. What's done is done. The most important thing is that you're here now and all you can do is try right your wrongs." Aunt Shirley turned back around and finished cooking her food.

Alyssa wiped her tears before she pulled out her phone to give Corey an update about her dad. When Aunt Shirley was finished preparing her fried fish and potatoes, she passed a plate to Alyssa, along with a glass of wine. They laughed as they ate, sipped, and talked. Although Aunt Shirley wasn't her favorite person in the world, she felt better after talking to her. The shots she fired at her about being an agent, putting her father in the hospital, and her hatred for her sister were nonstop, but the wine that was in her system made her laugh through it all. Alyssa being back at home was getting off to a great start. She just hoped it remained that way when she met up with the rest of her sisters and their mother.

Chapter 24

It had been a few days since Anastasia and Alyssa had beat Lizz down in the bathroom and she felt like a huge weight had been lifted off of her shoulders. Any bitch who would smile in your face and be fucking your man behind your back deserved an ass whooping and she was happy to have gotten a chance to do it; especially, since she had so much mouth before she realized that Alyssa was in the bathroom with them. Outside of the family bullshit with Lizz, Andrea had texted about daddy being sick, but Anastasia didn't know how serious it was, so she was waiting to hear from Alyssa because she really didn't want to go back to Mississippi.

She still had yet to hear from Richard, which she was both relieved and leery of that at the same time. While on the one hand she was happy that he wasn't bothering her, she still felt like at some point, he was going to pop up and try to wreak more havoc. The fact that Drea was in the background helping her out put her at ease a little bit, but for every victory she seemed to have gained, Richard came right in and shut that shit down. She looked back at her son as she drove him to school and said a silent prayer that things would go smoothly so that he wouldn't be negatively affected by any of the things that were going on. He still had yet to bring his father up and Anastasia knew it was because their relationship wasn't the best. Kyler obviously had her personality, because he was often turned off by how boring his father was, too. While Richard had always been a great father, as well as provider, he was never the type to play a video game, or wrestle around with their son.

The nigga couldn't even play basketball. She tried to fill that void for him as best she could, but she was still a woman and his mom, so most times, he wasn't feeling it the same way he would if it was a man. They pulled up to the school and she turned around smiling.

"Bye lil man," she cooed as he got his things prepared to get out of the car. He looked like a little man in his uniform, which was a white collared shirt, with a navy-blue sweater over it, and khaki pants. He pulled on his hat and his coat, then slipped the ninja turtle backpack on his back.

"Bye mom." He gave her a lazy grin and went to get out of the car, before stopping and looking back at her again, this time with a serious expression.

"When's my dad coming home?" The smile instantly dropped from her face and she was at a loss for words.

She couldn't help, but chastise herself mentally for not having something prepared for that question. Her eyes dropped briefly before she put on one of those looks mothers knew all too well. The facial expression that she wore said everything was okay, when in fact it wasn't.

"I'm not sure yet, honey. He's been pretty busy with work lately, but I'll make sure to call him and let him know that you want to see him," she said and the look on his face made her heart break and guilt washed over her.

She didn't think that it would bother him as much as it obviously was. Kyler nodded and smiled at her again as he got out of the car and ran into the school with the other kids. Once he'd disappeared into the building, she sighed heavily and pulled out her phone to unblock, and then call Richard.

"Hello," he answered on the first ring like he had been waiting on her call.

"Hi Richard, I'm calling because…"

"I knew it would only be a matter of time before you saw things my way," he boasted with a laugh and Anastasia pulled the phone away from her ear to look at it in disgust.

"Actually, I don't see anything your way! Your son wants to see you and I think you need to focus your energy on repairing your relationship with him and not on stopping this divorce!" she fussed and he got quiet all of a sudden.

"Is he upset with me?" He wanted to know back in father mode.

"No, I don't think that he's mad at you, I think he doesn't understand why someone he is used to seeing everyday has been missing for weeks."

"Well, it's not like that was my choice alone Anastasia!" he said sharply.

She couldn't argue with that. It was her decision to block Richard and hide her and her son from him. In her defense, at the time she felt like it was the best thing to do, but now seeing that Kyler missed his father, it was obvious that it wasn't the best for him.

"I know Richard, but you pushed me to do this!" she shrieked.

"All I want is a divorce, but you have threatened, blackballed, and did everything you can to stop me from getting that. Not to mention that you locked me out of my store!"

"We're not getting a divorce! It's clear that it's not what we need and it's no good for Kyler."

"Look, I'm just trying to talk to you about seeing Kyler that's it! But, the divorce is happening, Richard; whether you want it to or not!" Anastasia felt bad about the way their bullshit was affecting Kyler, but she was not going to stay in their marriage just to keep up an image, when she was unhappy and in love with someone else.

"I'm not about to argue with you, Ana, but I will be over to see our son later, and we can finish this discussion then." The phone beeped in her ear and she realized that he'd hung up on her.

She pinched the bridge of her nose and took a deep breath because the last thing she wanted to do was argue with him about whether or not they were getting a divorce. After a few minutes of sitting there and collecting herself, she headed home with a tight feeling in her gut.

Later that evening, she stood in the kitchen preparing Kyler's favorite meal, hamburger helper and sweet corn for dinner. She had to admit that she was nervous as hell about Richard bringing his crazy ass over, while Kyler bounced around happily. It helped a little bit that he was so excited about seeing his father, but she knew that once Kyler went to bed, Richard would start in with his bullshit about them being together.

The doorbell rang, and Kyler yelled and ran out of the kitchen before Anastasia could stop him.

"Ky, you better not answer that door!" she shouted, drying her hands on a towel and heading to the door herself. He stood right in the hallway shaking with excitement and she felt even worse seeing how bad he wanted to see Richard.

"Is it Dad? Is it?" He moved around her quickly trying to look through the curtain that covered the small window on the door.

"Boy, calm down!" Anastasia giggled and playfully swatted at him as she pulled open the door. Richard stood on the other side looking like he was about to ring the doorbell again. He must have come right over after work because he still had on his dress shirt, rolled up to the sleeve and pulled out of the navy slacks he wore. Their eyes met for a brief moment, and then Kyler jumped into his arms.

"Kyler, let him get in the house."

"It's alright, my sidekick missed me," Richard said, carrying him past her and into the house. She closed and locked the door and followed them into the living room.

"Well, I'm cooking, so I'll leave you two alone." She threw over her shoulder as she continued to the kitchen.

She could hear them laughing while she stirred the ground beef around in the skillet. The food was half done when she noticed that it had gotten really quiet. Turning around, she jumped seeing Richard standing on the other side of the island and staring at her intensely.

"Oh, my God, Richard!" She grabbed her chest and he chuckled.

"Sorry, I didn't mean to scare you."

"Where's Ky?" She wanted to know, not feeling comfortable being around him alone.

"He went to go get his iPad, so that he could show me some app on it." He shrugged and took a seat on one of the barstools.

"I figured I'd come talk to you for a minute while he was gone." She nodded and turned back to the stove, hoping to avoid a deep conversation, even though she was sure that's what he wanted.

"How have you been?" he asked, trying to feel Anastasia out.

She shrugged nonchalantly and waved a hand.

"I've been alright, I guess. Drea did text about daddy being sick, but I don't think it's anything serious." It was extremely weird for her that after all of the threats and crazy behavior that he had been displaying lately, that he could just come in asking casual questions like everything was okay. She didn't want to fight with him while Kyler was there, so she would play nice… for the time being.

"Lizz told me about what happened at the mall," he blurted out and she immediately froze up.

"So, what, you came over here to try and defend that hoe?" Turning around to face him she cocked her head to the side with all thoughts of not arguing gone.

"What! No, I was just letting you know that she told me. I'm not trying to defend anybody, but you need to understand that you and your sisters can't just go around putting your hands on people. She wanted to press charges!"

"And you should have let her! That would have been another beat down as soon as I saw her!" Anastasia growled.

She wished that bitch would be bold enough to try and go to the police when she had blatantly been fucking her husband. Lizz was lucky that all she did was fuck her up because for the disloyalty alone, she wanted to choke the life out of her.

Kyler entered the kitchen right then and Anastasia hurried to fix her facial expression. He looked between his parents as if he had heard them yelling, but then he smiled and ran over to his father with his tablet in his hand.

"Here's the game! We can go play it in the living room!" he gushed.

Anastasia turned back to the stove to let Richard know that the conversation was over. She hoped he got the hint and left the room with Kyler, because she was ready to curse him out. She finished the food not even 30 minutes later and called Kyler and Richard after setting their plates on the table in their usual spots. They both came walking into the kitchen hand-in-hand and took their seats ready to dig in. She made her plate slowly, and then joined them, hoping that they could get through the uncomfortable dinner in peace.

Things were going good. At least Richard hadn't said anything crazy the whole time he had been there. He and Kyler both had three helpings of hamburger helper, and by the time Kyler was finished, he was nodding off at the table. Richard laughed, which made Anastasia let out a chuckle of her own. She started to get up and get him ready for bed, but Richard waved her off and picked up their son and carried him to his room. She wanted to protest, but it honestly did feel nice to have some help. Sipping from her glass of wine, she rolled her eyes at D'Mani's name popping up on her phone. She peeked around the corner to make sure her husband wasn't coming and answered the phone, making sure to take the call towards the back of the house.

"What do you want, D'mani?"

"Damn, yo ass ain't talked to me in some fuckin' weeks, ma, And as soon as I get you on the phone, yo ass talkin' jazzy." he said in that smooth ass deep voice.

"You got some nerve, do you not remember me coming to your house and seeing you there with a woman!" she hissed so that Richard wouldn't hear her.

"Saw me with another woman?" he repeated sounding confused.

"Don't mock me! You know damn well what I'm talkin about!" she spat. That nigga knew full well what had happened. She didn't have time to play games with him, she was already going through enough and he was supposed to be her peace, but it seemed he was causing her just as much of a headache as her husband.

"You came to my house?"

"You know what! Fuck you, D'Mani! I'm already dealing with a lot right now and I really don't have time to raise you! So, why don't you get your mind right and don't hit me up until you do!" she told him, hanging up the phone before he could even say anything.

It was crazy that just a month before, nobody could tell her anything about how much D'Mani cared for her, but as time went on, it was starting to look a lot like bullshit. She pinched her nose, and then went back into the kitchen to finish eating. The fact that Richard was at the table staring off into space tweaked her out a little, but she didn't say anything and neither did he. His eyes narrowed at her with a look full of anger and he stood abruptly, leaving the kitchen and the house without saying a word. Anastasia already knew that he was listening as she talked to D'Mani. She just hoped he had enough sense not to go look for him. As Anastasia stood there, she began to think that going to Mississippi might be the best idea after all, since it was so much drama in New York.

Chapter 25

Anastasia quickly made her way through the airport with Kyler and their luggage in tow. She'd just arrived home for the Christmas holiday and she was ready to take a nap and make her son take one as well. The stress of the divorce, Richard's and D'Mani's behavior, and her sick father, was beginning to get the best of her; not to mention that she had just taken this same trip the week before. Since Thanksgiving, things just hadn't been going her way and she had not been handling it very well in her eyes. She hoped that she could get some relief from the things she was going through and at the same time, work on her relationship with her sisters and her mom and dad. Though she hadn't really been thinking about her father, Andrea's text saying that he was once again sick had her worried, though she tried not to show it. She sent a quick text to Drea letting her know that she had made it, and then went to the nearest car rental place. On the current trip, she didn't want to be stuck in one spot or depending on other people when she wanted to get around.

After receiving the keys to a Buick Verano, she loaded Kyler and their bags inside before heading to her childhood home. As she expected, her mother wasn't there and neither was anybody else. She figured she'd get herself situated, and then make a run up to the hospital to see her dad. Anastasia made her way upstairs to her old bedroom and put their things away before turning to ask Kyler if he was hungry, only to find him asleep on her bed. She should have known that he was as tired as she was or maybe even more so, since he hadn't really taken a nap. Climbing into bed with him, she sent a quick text to her sisters to let them know that she was at the house, but Kyler had fallen asleep, so she wouldn't be up to the hospital until later. She hadn't talked to Alyssa yet to see if she'd made it, but she could do that when she woke up. At the moment, all she wanted to do was catch some shut-eye while Kyler was down. She was out as soon as her head hit the pillow.

Anastasia woke up to the loud sounds of no other than her Aunt Shirley and immediately wanted to close her eyes right back. She planned to do just that, but noticed that Kyler was no longer beside her. The last thing she wanted was him spending too much time alone with that crazy old drunk; especially, after she tried to say that Zyree was his father. Knowing her Aunt, she'd try and do a damn home DNA test on him. With that thought in mind, she hurried down the stairs to find all of her sisters and her Aunt sitting in the living room. Drea and Lexi were sitting on the loveseat while Lyssa, Aunt Shirley sat on the couch, and Kyler sat in the middle of the floor, playing a basketball game with a guy Anastasia could only assume was one of Alexis's new boo's. She stopped at the bottom of the stairs and watched for a minute at how excited he got when he scored a point and the guy gave him a dap.

"Hey hoe!" Lexi's voice brought her out of her thoughts and all eyes landed on her as she came further into the room.

"Hi Alexis." Anastasia rolled her eyes at her little sister before greeting everyone else, and then taking a seat next to Alyssa. Kyler was so engrossed in the game that he didn't even look up, he just mumbled a hello along with the rest of the room and kept right on playing.

"Who's he?" she asked her sister quietly, nodding in the direction of the mystery guy.

"Oh, that's me and Lexi new boo thang," Aunt Shirley attempted to whisper with a wink, causing Stasia and Alyssa to laugh.

"Aunty, I ain't gone tell you again!" Lexi said from across the room with a smile. Aunt Shirley shrugged her shoulders and took a sip of the flask she was holding like she didn't care about nothing Lexi was saying.

"Girl, stop being so stingy all the time damn!" she snapped and rolled her eyes. Lexi didn't say anything and Anastasia was sure because she knew that he wasn't at all interested. After all of the laughter died down from Aunt Shirley's silliness, he turned to Stasia slightly and stuck out a hand.

"Since yo sister being all rude and what not, hi I'm Jeremy, but everybody calls me J.R." he said.

"Nice to meet you, I'm Anastasia," she told him, slipping her hand into his. She had to admit that he was a nice-looking guy and he had much better manners than some of the niggas Alexis had introduced them to. Anastasia was impressed.

"Boy, I am not rude!" Lexi quipped from the other couch and he gave her a look like she was lying before they all burst into laughter. Everyone knew Alexis was the rudest of the Holiday sisters and that was mostly because of Aunt Shirley. J.R. returned to the game and Anastasia looked to her sisters.

"So, how's dad doing?" She asked praying that he was okay.

She may not have had the best relationship with her father, but she loved him and cared about his health. Drea filled her in on what was going on and the visit they all had today, putting her at ease a little bit, even though she still was worried. They discussed their plans to see him again the next day and Anastasia was all for it; especially, since she didn't get the chance to earlier.

"Ya'll wanna go grab a bite? I swear I'm starving," Drea said after they'd had been sitting silently for a while.

"Bitch, of course you starving, you got my neicey or nephy poos up in there," Alexis laughed and rubbed her belly while Andrea rolled her eyes.

"I could eat something, me and Ky didn't even eat before we fell asleep earlier." Anastasia looked over at Alyssa who nodded her agreement.

With his eyes still on the game, Kyler finally said something since he'd greeted her when she came in the room.

"I want Pizza!" he shouted gleefully.

"I'm down for some pizza too nephew, but you gotta put the game and everything away so you can get ready to go," Alexis let him know patiently.

"We can't order it here?" Anastasia knew he would put up a little fight to stay there. If there was a video game involved, Kyler didn't move much.. She'd watched him sit for an hour or more trying to win a whole game before.

"Nah lil homie, we gone take the ladies out, but after that we can come back and finish playing. Cool?" the guy J.R. asked and Kyler readily agreed. Anastasia directed him upstairs so that he could get his shoes and other things while she and her sisters gathered themselves. He came running back into the living room with his shoes and coat on way faster than she expected him to.

"Y'all ready?" Drea asked everyone in the room, slipping into her jacket and heading to the door after they all nodded that they were.

"So, y'all just wasn't gone invite me, huh?" Aunt Shirley, who was walking out last, asked with her hands on her hips.

"Now, Aunt Shirley, you know you was coming." Alexis laughed, ushering her forward.

"I better had of been... lil rude ass hoes," She griped in a low voice that she knew everybody heard.

"Yo, your Aunty wild as hell," JR told Lexi with a grin. It was good to see that he could roll with the punches when it came to Aunt Shirley because her mouth truly had no filter. Him, Alexis, and Aunt Shirley got into the car with Andrea, while Alyssa and Kyler got into the car with Stasia.

The drive over to Pizza Hut didn't take long at all and Anastasia caught up with her sister, but she could tell that she was holding something in. Anastasia hoped that it wasn't Corey because she didn't wasn't to have to cut his ass. She figured she would ask her sister about it later, because they were already pulling up to the restaurant. They parked right next to Drea since the lot wasn't full and everyone got out. Kyler ran ahead, so that he could walk in with Alexis and her boyfriend and Anastasia was glad that he took a liking to J.R. because she was a firm believer that if kids didn't like you, something was probably wrong with you.

She stood next to Alyssa and laughed at how Aunt Shirley was swaying like she was about to fall over. It didn't help that she was dressed in some high-waist jeans with a collared shirt and a jean jacket. They made jokes as she attempted to flirt with J.R. while Lexi shook her head, and Andrea spoke to the hostess.

They were led to a long table so that they could all eat together, and then they placed their drink orders. Since, almost everybody wanted something different they got pepperoni, sausage, cheese, and some kind of vegetable pizza that Anastasia had no interest in. The conversation flowed and surprisingly, they were able to get along without there being any words. Unfortunately, for Anastasia, that didn't last long because Zyree came out of nowhere and Aunt Shirley made it a point to call him over to their table. He looked confused at first because he probably didn't remember her, but his face lit up once he got close enough to see Stasia. She made sure to cut her eyes at her Aunt who only shrugged like she wasn't trying to start some shit.

"Hey Stasia, hey holiday sisters," he joked once he stood over the table. Him and J.R. shook hands and greeted each other while everyone else said hi.

"Hi Zyree," Stasia mumbled and pushed Kyler's tablet toward him, so that he was occupied.

"This yo baby?" He wanted to know eyeing her son and making her feel uncomfortable.

"Uhh…. yeah... Zyree, this is Kyler. Kyler, this is mommy's friend, Zyree," she introduced the two. Kyler looked up briefly and waved, then hurried to return to his game. Zyree never took his eyes off of him until Anastasia cleared her throat.

"How old is he?"

Even though she didn't want to tell him for fear that he would think the same thing as her Aunt, she still took a deep breath and then mumbled five. Zyree's eyes bucked, and then narrowed back down to Kyler.

"So that means…?" his voice trailed off so as not to say what she knew he was thinking.

"No! No Zyree… he's not." He looked like he didn't believe her and again, she cut her eyes at her Aunt.

"Don't be looking at me! You know that count is off!" Aunt Shirley chuckled while her sisters all looked on confused. Well, all except Drea, she had been up the night that Anastasia snuck out.

"I told you that he's not his father," Stasia hissed and cut her eyes at Kyler to be sure that he was still engrossed in his game, thankfully he was.

"That don't make it true." She pointed out with her head cocked like she dared her to argue.

"Anastasia, I have somewhere to be, but I definitely intend to talk about this with you later," he said, stealing her attention, and then leaving after he got another good look at Kyler.

As soon as he was away from the table, they all turned to look at Anastasia.

"Well?" Lexi asked, taking the same stance as her Aunt.

"Well what, Alexis?"

"Bitch is he uh… you know?" She tilted her head at Kyler, who still had yet to pay any of them any attention.

"No! He's not! Just drop it please?" she begged, looking back down into her plate. It looked like she had another dilemma. If there was any truth to Zyree's words and knowing him, he fully intended to on following-up with her.

"Okay, okay." She held up both hands in surrender.

"But, I don't think he gone drop it."

"Unfortunately," Anastasia grumbled in irritation. Her night had officially been ruined, just when she thought that things were going good this time, some more shit had popped up.

Chapter 26

Their dad was doing much better, the sisters were getting along, and it was finally feeling like Christmas. Andrea hated that their dad got sick again, but she was happy to have her sister's home and she knew that was the only reason they were there. It hadn't been any real drama and she was thankful for that and prayed that it stayed that way. She got up early Saturday morning and thought about cooking a little breakfast for Lexi and J.R., but quickly dismissed that thought. Knowing Lexi, they were up and gone anyway because it was a little after ten. Andrea was actually a little tired and needed to rest her body. Between going back and forth to the hospital and still trying to work the past week, she was tired. When she left work the day before, she wouldn't be returning until after the New Year and she was happy about it.

Andrea's phone rang and she knew that it was her girl by the *Best Friend* by Brandy ringtone. She rolled over and grabbed the phone off of the nightstand and slid it to answer.

"Girrrlllll, are you resting up for your big day?" Hannah sang.

"Big day? Hannah, are you high this morning?"

"I wish… but, bitch D gonna be here today. Remember?"

"Ohhhh shit!! That is today… Oh my gawwddd!!"

"Drea, you forgot the damn man was flying in from New York? Shame on you!"

"Umm... you know everything that's been going on. Hell, sometimes I be forgetting I'm pregnant, so a baby daddy wasn't nowhere near my mind."

"Yeah, that's understandable... how's Mr. Abraham before I continue?" Hannah quizzed.

"Much better... thank God!!" Drea exclaimed.

"Great... now we gotta get you ready for your baby daddy. What y'all gon do? He coming to your house?"

"I really don't know. I don't know how I forgot about this. You think I should let him come here?"

"You pregnant by the nigga now... ain't no shy stage no more hell."

"Shut up Hannah!"

While her friend was rambling, Drea put her on speaker and checked her text messages. Sure enough, D had texted her and said that his flight was scheduled to land fifteen minutes after two. Shit was about to get real in a few short hours and Drea was nervous as hell.

"Are you listening to me?" Hannah yelled.

"Nah... I was reading a text message. What you say?"

"I said you really should cook him a nice meal, and then fuck him good."

"Hannah!!!!"

"What? You already pregnant! I know you ain't gon make the nigga fly down here for nothing hell... the fuck!!"

Andrea couldn't do nothing, but laugh at her crazy ass friend. Whatever popped into Hannah's mind, nine times outta ten, the shit came out. She had to admit, that was one of the things she loved about her though. Realness was rare these days, so if you met a real person, it would be wise to keep them close.

"Shut the hell up, Hannah... whatever happens, happens... but, that's not in my plans."

"Whatever you say... you need me to come over and help with anything?"

"If I think of anything, I'll let you know," Drea laughed and hung up.

Hannah's comment had her once again thinking about the bomb ass sex that she had shared with D in New York and the possibility of getting some again did make her wet. Instead of pulling out her vibrator, she got out of the bed and made her way into the bathroom to relieve her bladder and handle her hygiene. Drea stayed in the shower almost thirty minutes because the water was feeling so good on her body. After she dried off, she threw on some tights and a collegiate tee, and then did her hair. Her sew in was still intact and she was thankful. After applying some Hicks edge control and brushing her baby hairs, and doing her eye brows, she was good to go.

Andrea made her way to the kitchen to see what she had that she could whip up for D. it was almost one o'clock by then, so she knew she had to pick up the pace. Thankfully, she hadn't been too long went grocery shopping and as she made her way to the kitchen, she had pretty much decided on Gumbo. The only thing that she needed to make sure she had was some Worcestershire sauce because she knew she had everything else. Drea had learned to stock her cabinets with seasonings just like her mother. She found it right away and was glad that she wasn't going to have to leave out.

After pulling out everything she needed, it was a little after one and Andrea connected her phone to her Bose speaker and turned a holiday station on. She texted Lexi to see where she was, just to get an idea of how long she was going to be gone, and Lexi told her that she probably wouldn't be back until later that night. She heated and stirred the flour to form a roux for about thirty minutes. As *Silent Night* by the Temptations was playing, she added the onions, bell pepper, celery, garlic, and okra. She skipped adding beer since she was pregnant, and she didn't have any at her house anyway, and mixed in bay leaves, cayenne, salt, Worcestershire, and a few other seasonings and let it simmer for about an hour.

Her phone rang as she took the shrimp, fish, and oysters out to add in later, and her stomach formed in knots when she saw that it was D calling. She answered before he hung up.

"What's up, baby mama?" he chuckled and eased Drea's nerves instantly.

His voice did something to her that was unexplainable.

"What's up, baby daddy?"

"I just landed. Where you wanna meet at?"

"Actually, I'm cooking some Gumbo, so you can come here. I'll text you my address."

"Cool cool... my brother wit me, but Ima drop him off at the Hilton and I'll be there soon.

"Sounds good, but he can come if he wants to."

"That nigga will be aight for now."

"Well okay then," Drea said, and then hung up.

She texted him her address as soon as she ended the call, and then went to check on her food. Drea finally added the meats, and parsley, and took some rice out to cook, but she would wait a little while before she cooked it. She couldn't believe that she was really about to be face to face with her mystery man again. What was supposed to be a one night stand had quickly turned into something else. Drea wasn't sure exactly what it was, but it was damn sure something. Her phone rang again and it was Hannah. She had Drea laughing so hard that she started crying. They talked and talked and she never realized how much time had passed by until D beeped in and told her that he was pulling up. Drea clicked over without telling Hannah to hold on or anything.

She hurriedly put some water in a boiler for the rice, and as soon as she added a dash of salt to the water, her doorbell rang. As she walked to the front door, Drea realized that she never changed clothes.

"Damn," she mumbled, but continued forward.

When she opened the door, there stood the man that she had dreamt about on countless nights. He was looking sexy as ever and Drea didn't realize that she was biting her lips until she felt the slight sting.

"I'm sorry... come on in," she finally said.

D walked in and pulled her in for a hug and Drea melted in his arms. The scent of his Polo Red cologne filled her nostrils and drew her in even more. When he finally released her, he bent down and gave her a quick, but sensual kiss that made her knees buckle.

"Damn... you done took my mind all the way left," Drea laughed when she backed away from him and made her way to the kitchen.

"Make yourself at home," she said as went in the kitchen to put the rice into the boiling water.

"You looking good in them tights, ma."

"I really meant to change."

"Nah, you good... everything is so natural about you. I like that."

His comment made her blush. Their conversation flowed so freely and it seemed as if they had known each other forever. When the rice was done, Drea made bowls for both of them and sat them on the table. They sat down and out of habit, she said grace before they ate. Their dad always made them say a prayer before taking a bite of anything and that was something that stuck even as an adult. Drea knew that she could throw down in the kitchen, but she was nervous as hell as she waited to see what D thought about what she had whipped up.

"This shit slamming. What's this called?" he quizzed.

"It's Gumbo. I used a recipe that I got from one of my friends in Louisiana years ago."

"Never even heard of that, but it's good as hell."

They talked about everything under the son and Drea found out a lot about D and his family. She thought that when it was time to talk about the babies, things would get awkward, but surprisingly they didn't. D didn't have any kids and he seemed very excited.

"I know this ain't how normal shit is supposed to go, but it really was something about you. I honestly never thought I would see you again, but I'm glad that I did. You just got this chill ass vibe that I like," he expressed.

"I really feel the same way. I'm ashamed to admit how many times I've thought about you… and that's before AND after I reached out to you."

"You want some more?" she asked when she saw that his bowl was empty.

"Yeah, I'll take some more."

Drea grabbed his bowl and got up and went into the kitchen. Before she could fix him another serving, D walked up behind her and grabbed her waist. He nibbled on her neck and her whole body began to tingle. D moved his hands up her body and they landed on her breasts. He squeezed them through her shirt and soft moans escaped her lips. Drea turned around and as soon as she did, their lips met and he kissed her feverishly. D picked her up and put her on the counter, all the while, his tongue never left her mouth. She wrapped her legs tightly around him as her juices began to flow. D pulled her shirt over her head, unsnapped her bra, and then sucked her breasts one at a time with intensity.

Andrea fumbled with his jeans and finally unbuckled his belt. As soon as her mission was accomplished, he lifted her up a little and pulled her tights and panties down. She knew that he was about to give her exactly what she wanted and needed. As soon as he entered her, they both moaned.

"Damn… this pussy tight just like I remember it," D grunted as he glided in and out of her.

He was feeling better than Drea remembered and she felt like she was in heaven. She pulled him close and squeezed her pelvic muscles tight. When she did that, it seemed to send D over the edge. His body began to shake and so did hers.

"You want me to pull out?"

"I'm already pregnant," she replied and they both laughed.

"Let it go, ma," he coaxed her.

Those words were like music to her ears. Drea's body began to shake and she pulled D close to her. As soon as her juices began to flow, he grunted and they came at the same time.

"Damn girl… you gon make me move to country ass Mississippi, so I can live in this pussy," he chuckled.

"You damn shol can live in it," she confirmed.

Drea hopped down off the counter and made her way to the bathroom. She called out to D and he followed.

"Round 2?" he quizzed.

"Don't tempt me. I'm tryna give you a towel to clean up," she told him.

"When are you leaving?"

"Monday evening. I figured we could spend as much time together as possible, ya know."

"I'd like that," she smiled.

"Okay... let's go get you those seconds, and then we'll see about round two," Drea said after they finished cleaning up.

Chapter 27

Staying at Drea's house turned out to be better than Lexi had expected. It reminded her of the old days when she would sneak into Drea's room and sleep with her because she had a bad dream. The only complaint was that her and J.R. had to fuck in silence because Drea's room was so close to the guest room, but when Drea would leave the crib, they would go crazy! They had been in Mississippi since last Sunday. It was the next Saturday and surprisingly, Lexi wasn't ready to kill her sisters or go back home. She went to the hospital every single day to visit her father and was happy to report that he was doing better. Mr. Holiday's surgery was scheduled for Monday morning, which was Christmas day. The only Christmas miracle she wished for, was for father to recover so things could go back to normal.

Although Lexi grew up in the church, her faith as an adult somewhat shifted. She still believed in all the Christians values that she was taught, it's just that the older she got, the less she talked to God. But, with the health scare her father was facing, she had been speaking with him on a regular lately. Last Sunday, the day she arrived in Mississippi, Lexi introduced J.R. to her mother and Mrs. Holiday welcomed him with opened arms. She would never tell her mom that they were living together because that would send her to the hospital next. She didn't even let her know that he was staying at Drea's house either. She thought that he was crashing at a hotel and was there for support. Honestly, Lexi felt that her mom couldn't care less, as long as her baby girl wasn't gay. Mrs. Holiday was happy to hear that Lexi stopped dancing, but was shocked when she found out that J.R. was the reason. That alone had Mrs. Holiday talking about marriage, but of course Lexi wasn't trying to hear that shit.

"You really finna wait on your auntie?" J.R. asked as he rolled the second blunt from the driver side of his truck.

"Yeah, that's my G and I always blow with her," she replied, looking out the window to see if Aunt Shirley was coming down the street yet.

"Y'all one fucked up family. Ya pops a preacher and ya moms this wholesome ass house wife who sister smokes with her youngest child," J.R. broke it down.

"Well, now that you put it that way, I guess shit is a little off."

"A little, huh?" J.R. replied followed by a cough as he hit the blunt.

They chatted for a few more minutes before Shirley finally made her way inside the truck.

"Ohhh weee! That shit smells good!" she said, getting in the backseat.

Both J.R. and Lexi laughed before they passed her the blunt. The entire car smoked in silence. Lexi reflected on life while J.R. and Shirley was thinking about whatever it was they was thinking about.

"Aye bae!" Aunt Shirley said from the backseat.

Lexi and J.R. looked at each other and broke out in laughter.

"Who you talking to, Auntie?" Lexi asked.

"Our bae, J.R. You know I'm talking to you," she informed the both of them.

"What's up, Auntie?" he asked.

"You do know that I use to look just like Lexi in my younger days and I know damn well I can ride a dick better than her."

"AUNTIE.... CHILL MAN..... DAMN!" Lexi said, actually getting irritated with her Auntie and her no filter having ass.

"It's cool baby," J.R. laughed, rubbing Lexi's knee.

"Girl, ain't nobody trying to take yo man," Aunt Shirley replied.

"But, I can!" she continued, winking her eye at Lexi, who turned around in her seat.

"So, nephew.... Imma call you nephew since I can't call you bae. Where yo daddy at?" she asked, taking a sip from her flask.

J.R. ignored her and passed her the second blunt that was in rotation now. The three of them smoked until they couldn't smoke anymore. Lexi noticed Alyssa and Anastasia getting out the car and going inside her parents' house just as they exited J.R.'s truck

"We can smell that shit from over here," Stasia yelled from the porch.

"Maybe you should take a hit, bitch.... Loosen yo bougie ass up a little bit," Lexi replied, mumbling the last part.

"You better say that shit!" Aunt Shirley laughed, slapping high-fives with Lexi.

Lexi's sister and Aunt Shirley went inside her parent's house while her and J.R. headed over to Drea's. She knew that she had to come down off her high a little bit before being around her mom. Lexi went inside her purse and pulled out the spare key Drea had given her and entered the house. When she walked in, the smell of Gumbo smacked her in the face, causing her stomach to growl instantly. She was high and had the munchies. Drea's famous Gumbo was going to hit the spot. Lexi and J.R. headed towards the kitchen, but the both of them stopped in their tracks when Drea and some fine ass man was coming out of the bathroom.

"Shit! I'm sorry, are we interrupting?" Lexi said with a devilish grin plastered on her face.

"No child! Lexi and J.R., this is my ummmmmm friend, D. D, this is my sister and soon to be brother in law J.R.," she said, introducing everybody.

"What's up, homie?" J.R. spoke first while Lexi stood there grinning.

"Nice to meet you, Mr. D," Lexi finally replied.

"Yeah, D is here from New York," Drea stated.

"Ohhhh this is D…. The D that put down the "D"," Lexi burst out laughing at her own joke.

The three of them joined in before Lexi pulled J.R. away. All that talking about "D" made her want some, so she pulled him into the room and started undressing. Without warning, Lexi pulled her shirt over her head, slipped out of her UGGs, followed by her pants. Once she made it down to her panties, she noticed that J.R. was sitting on the edge of the bed with a blank stare.

"What's wrong?" she asked, walking over to him, taking a seat on his lap.

After a few seconds of silence, he finally spoke, "Who is buddy in the living room?"

"Aw, that's Drea's baby daddy. Her thot ass went to New York, had a one night stand and ended up pregnant by him. That shit crazy, right?" Lexi rambled on, but J.R.'s facial expression never changed.

"He from New York?"

"Yeah, why baby?" Lexi questioned.

"Aye hold up!" He lifted Lexi up off his lap slightly before going inside his pocket, pulling out his phone.

Lexi watched on as he texted someone, a few seconds later his phone chimed, indicating he had a new text message. J.R. read whatever was sent to him before yelling, "FUCK!"

"What's wrong? What happened?" a worried Lexi inquired.

"Remember when I told you that I had to go to New York to take care of some business?"

Instead of replying, Lexi nodded her head up and down.

"Well it turns out that your sister baby daddy is the nigga I gotta handle," he stated, showing Lexi a picture on his phone, a picture of the same nigga that Drea had just introduced them to.

Chapter 28

Christmas Eve

Alyssa woke up early Christmas Eve morning filled with the Christmas spirit. She jumped out of bed and headed to the bathroom to handle her hygiene before getting dressed for the day. Yoga pants, a tank top, and a pair of slippers was her outfit of choice. She grabbed the wrapping paper and began wrapping the presents she purchased for her family. Alyssa couldn't wait to see the looks on her family faces when they opened their gifts.

When she was finished with the gifts, she carried them downstairs and placed them under the tree. After the last gift was tucked away, Alyssa began to cook brunch for the family. She wanted to get her family into the Christmas spirit as well, but she wanted to see if her family would notice what she was up to. She was in the middle of mixing the batter for the waffles when Kyler entered the kitchen with a pouty face. She watched him as he flopped down in a nearby chair and folded his arms across his chest. She chuckled at the sight of him and couldn't help but wonder what was wrong.

"Are you okay, nephew?"

"No. Mommy won't let me see my gifts until tomorrow."

"Aww. Well, maybe I can convince your mom to let you open a gift tonight, okay?" she smiled.

"Okay!" he cheered up instantly.

"In the meantime, would you like to help me cook?"

"Yeah!"

Alyssa and Kyler's conversation, laughter, and aroma of the food drew everyone from their rooms and into the kitchen. The holiday sisters, Victoria and J.R., eyed Alyssa suspiciously as they watched them cook.

"Alyssa, what is going on in here?" Victoria quizzed.

"I'm just preparing brunch for everyone. Nothing special. Is something wrong with that, mom?" she smirked.

"You ain't fooling nobody, Lyssa. The Holiday tradition is in full effect." Andrea smiled.

"The holiday tradition? Anastasia asked with a raised eyebrow.

"Damn. It's been years since we did that. What made you think of that?" Lexi took a seat at the table.

"Well, I figured since we're all home, we could celebrate Christmas like we used to. I know dad isn't here to be a part of the festivities, but I think it would make him happy that his family is celebrating the holiday the right way and not fighting." She eyed everyone in the kitchen.

"I hate to admit it, but she's right," Andrea nodded.

Everyone nodded their heads in agreement, which put a smile on Alyssa's face.

"Aight. Let's get started, but nobody better not touch ANY of my gifts." Lexi pointed at her sisters.

They shared a laugh before they began to set the table. Alexis filled J.R. in on the Holiday Tradition and what it was as well as its meaning. After giving him the run down, he nodded his head in understanding. The house was full of the Christmas spirit and there was nothing but good vibes floating around and it reminded Alyssa of when they were younger.

Every Christmas Eve, they would wake up and eat brunch before their mother prepared dinner. They would also bake Christmas cookies, watch movies, and open one of their gifts before they went to sleep and Alyssa wanted to relive all of those memories. When the food was finished, Alyssa placed everything on the table and before they all sat down, Aunt Shirley walked in.

"Well, check y'all out. I was prepared to whoop some ass so I could get y'all into the Christmas spirit, but I see someone done got the ball rollin'." She took a seat at the table.

"I brought some eggnog to livin' things up around here." Aunt Shirley placed two containers on the table.

"Aunt Shirley, this one is almost empty." Anastasia shook one of the containers.

"I got started early." She lifted her flask and winked at her.

Alyssa chuckled at her Aunt.

"Ummm, before we eat, I just want to apologize for the way I've been behavin'," Victoria spoke up.

"I'm not goin' to lie and say that I'm happy with the decisions you girls made, but y'all are still my daughters and I love y'all dearly. I'm very worried about your father, but I know that his surgery is goin' to be just fine. I'm glad that y'all are here with me durin' this tryin' time. I know I can be stubborn, but I need y'all right now." Victoria began to sob.

Alexis jumped up to console her mother, while the others told her that it wasn't a problem. After a brief prayer, they didn't hesitate to dig into their food. Alyssa's phone chimed letting her know she had a text and she checked it immediately. She was a bit disappointed when she saw it was Tara texting her instead of Corey, but she didn't let that put a damper on her mood.

They sat around the table telling embarrassing stories about the girls' childhood. Like when Alyssa had to be rushed to the hospital for sticking beads up her nose and how Anastasia got her ass whooped because Lexi lied and said Stasia broke her favorite toy. Aunt Shirley told a story of how Andrea pissed on herself when she took her to a haunted house for Halloween, that made everyone laugh until their stomachs hurt. The women shared stories and laughs as they ate for about an hour and none of them were too concerned that a man was at the table or that they sat there longer than intended, until Alyssa announced it was time to move on to the next tradition.

Andrea and Alyssa cleared the table before washing the dishes. Alyssa expressed to her older sister how excited she was about the twins and how much she was going to spoil them. Andrea inquired about Corey and she informed him that he would be making an appearance some time that day. The holiday sisters had been getting along quite well since they all arrived and it felt like they were starting to form a bond they never had.

They all stayed in the kitchen sipping eggnog as they prepared to cook dinner and bake Christmas cookies. Anastasia pulled the Christmas shaped cookie cutters from the drawer while Aunt Shirley, Victoria, and Lexi cooked the food. Kyler seemed to be enjoying himself as he helped his mom with the cookies. Andrea pulled out her phone and provided the house with some Christmas jams and when *I*

Saw Mommy Kissing Santa Claus by the Jackson 5 came through the speaker, they all sang along to the music while they danced. J.R. watched the women carry on for a few minutes before he excused himself to the living room. Everyone had smiles on their faces and that holiday feeling that Alyssa was trying to recreate had finally made it presence in the house. Alyssa didn't want to tell her family about her suspension, but she was tired of being secretive and she wanted her family to know the truth about her job. So, she told them what happened to her and how she was under investigation. They all stared at her with wide eyes as she confirmed what everyone was thinking, which was that their father was right about law enforcement, but instead of harsh remarks, they consoled her.

As the day went on, Alyssa stepped away from the family to call Corey a few times, but his phone went straight to voicemail. Each failed attempt made her anger grow a little more, but she managed to hide it. They communicated throughout the week and he reminded her that he would be there. So, she didn't understand why he hadn't arrived yet. After she made the last failed call to Corey, Kyler found her on the porch and informed her that dinner was ready. His excitement made her cheer up a little as he dragged her to the kitchen table to eat.

After filling their bellies with cornbread, collard greens, fried chicken, honey ham, string beans, and Mac and cheese later that evening, Aunt Shirley and Victoria put the food up while the girls gathered around the Christmas tree to open their gifts. As *Santa Claus Goes Straight To the Ghetto* by James Brown played in the background, Alyssa handed each of her sisters their gifts as she let Kyler chose from one of the three she purchased for him. She watched as they all opened their gifts from her and the looks on their faces were priceless.

"Damn Alyssa, these bracelets are the shit." Andrea admired her Pandora charm bracelet with the "HS" charms on it.

"Yeah, Lyssa. I think this is one of the nicest gifts you ever got me." Lexi placed the bracelet on her wrist.

"Let's be real. That's the ONLY gift she ever brought your ass," Anastasia stated.

They all laughed.

"Wow! Autie Lyssa brought me a PS4 and the latest games!! Thank you!!" He squeezed her tightly.

"You're welcome, baby." She kissed his cheek.

"How you get these raggedy heffas gifts and didn't get me anythin'?" Aunt Shirley entered the living room.

Alyssa reached under the tree and grabbed her aunts gift and handed it to her. As she waited for Aunt Shirley to open her gift, the doorbell rang. No one seemed to be worried about the doorbell so, she answered the door. Alyssa opened the door without looking through the peephole and when she saw it was Corey, she jumped on him causing him to stumble back on the porch.

"Oh, my goodness. You don't know how much I missed you." She closed her eyes and squeezed him tighter as his hand cuffed her ass.

"I missed you, too, bae."

They shared a passionate kiss that lasted for a few minutes. Corey placed Alyssa on her feet, but she kept her arms wrapped around his neck.

"What took you so long?"

"It took me awhile to pick up ya Christmas gift," he smirked at her.

"What gift?"

Corey stepped to the side and a black 2018 Cadillac Escalade was parked in front of the house with a red bow on it. Her mouth flew open as she rushed down the porch steps to examine the car. Alyssa shrieked when she opened the door and saw all the features that the car came with. She knew Corey was going to get her something for Christmas, but a new car wasn't what she had in mind.

"I love you so much, baby! Thank you!" She kissed him again.

"It took you all day to get this?"

"Yeah. I bought it at one of the dealerships down here. I was gonna get you the car when we got back to the NY, but you need a gift a now and don't worry, I'll have your truck shipped home," he chuckled.

"Good because I'll be damned if I'm leaving my truck down here," she stated seriously.

"Oh, and about that baby thing, it was scam," he stated with confidence.

"What you mean a scam?"

"Shawty sent me a text talkin' about the baby ain't mine and the only reason she accused me of bein' the father is because her nigga got booked and she didn't want to raise the baby alone." He pulled out his phone and showed Alyssa the text.

She took her time reading the message his fling sent him and he was indeed telling the truth. The chick said that she felt bad setting him up like that and apologized for her actions. Alyssa handed him back his phone with a smile on her face. She threw her arms around him again hugging him tighter than before.

"So, when is that date for the weddin' again?"

"I wanted to get married in the spring, but I want to get married sooner than that. We can go to the justice of the peace to get married and the ceremony later."

"That works for me because I can't wait another day to have you as my wife."

"But, let this be known, if you cheat on me again, you're going to either end up in a hospital or in a grave. Do you hear me?"

Corey bit his lip before he peaked hers, letting her know that he understood her.

"Get a damn room you two," Anastasia yelled from the screen door.

"Stasia, call the family out here so they can see my new truck." Alyssa pointed

Anastasia shouted to the family to come outside and they all came out the door one by one. Corey greeted Victoria with a hug and a kiss on the cheek and he greeted her sisters the same way. Alyssa introduced Corey to J.R. and they shook hands before Corey wrapped his arms around her waist. Alexis didn't hesitate to hop her ass behind the wheel of her truck, leaving the door open. After she got finished checking out her truck, she told Alyssa that she looked good behind the wheel and that Alyssa should let her borrow the truck. She dismissed Lexi with a hand wave and she motioned for everyone to come back inside.

Aunt Shirley thanked Alyssa for her rose gold customized flask and the bottle of whiskey as they made their way into the living room to watch movies. *Home Alone*, a classic holiday movie, was just coming on as they all got comfortable in their seats.

As Corey and Alyssa snuggled on the couch, she couldn't help but to recap her day. The day she planned was a success and it made her feel like it was a step in the right direction for their future as a family. The love and good vibes that flowed throughout the house was different for her and her sisters, as well as their mother. Reliving the Holiday Tradition was to get them to forget their differences towards each other and to remember what it was like to be a family. She wanted to build the foundation for an unbreakable bond for the four of them and felt that she accomplished that. Alyssa secretly wanted a relationship with Andrea and Alexis, but was too stubborn to take that step until that day. They say that miracles happened on Christmas and Alyssa was in agreement because the day she just endured with her family and the news about Corey's fling was proof of that. The last miracle that she needed to happen was for their father to return home in a healthy and happy state.

Chapter 29

Just when Lexi began to get into the holiday spirit, Ebenezer Scrooge came along and fucked things up. The time she spent with her family yesterday was amazing, but she couldn't get her mind off the fact that her boyfriend had plans on killing her sister's baby daddy. The saying "small world" never hit home until right then. Lexi laid in the bed fidgeting with the neckless that Alyssa had given to her as a gift the night before. Her and her sisters never exchanged gifts as adults and she didn't expect them to this year either, which made Lexi relieved that she went ahead and got them something too.

"Wake y'all asses up and MERRY CHRISTMAS!" Drea yelled, followed by three hard knocks on the bedroom door.

J.R. stirred in his sleep while Lexi attempted to get out the bed.

"Why the fuck y'all wake up so early around here?" he asked in a groggy voice.

Lexi grabbed her phone off the nightstand to look at the time, "It's 8:00 a.m., it's not that early; besides, it Christmas morning. Get up!"

Lexi went inside the connecting bathroom and hopped in the shower. After she was done, she rambled through a Target bag and pulled out the Christmas sweater that she recently purchased. She laid it across the bed along with some black leggings. She then grabbed the black Christian Louboutin peep toe boots she brought with her and placed them on the floor next to the bed. By the time she was done lotioning up and applying her make-up, J.R. walked out of the shower with the towel wrapped around his waist. Lexi admired his fit frame, which caused her pussy to get wet instantly. She watched him grab his MCM duffle bag and pull out a pair of ripped up Balmain jeans with a Gucci collar shirt to match.

"Wait. Wait. Wait. I forgot to show you what I brought for you," Lexi said, getting up from where she was sitting and going back over to the closet, pulling out a Christmas sweater for him.

"What's that?" J.R. asked, eyeing her.

"When we were younger, we all got dressed up in Christmas sweaters on Christmas day," she explained, handing him the sweater.

"Well, good thing I ain't a part of this family," he replied, tossing the shirt back to her.

"Jerrreeeemmmmyyyy pleeeaassseeee!" she whined, poking out her bottom lip.

"Allleexxiiissss noooooooooo!" he mocked her while he pulled the Gucci shirt over his head.

"You dead ass ain't gon wear it?" she asked, getting upset.

"I'm dead ass not wearing that ugly ass sweater," he informed her.

"Whatever, FUCK IT!" she snapped, tossing the sweater back in the bag.

"Bruh, don't nobody give no fuck cuz you mad over some stupid shit."

"We know, you don't give a fuck about nothing."

"And what that supposed to me Lexi?" he asked.

"Nothing man, let's just get dressed."

The couple got dressed in silence. That was not how Lexi planned on starting her Christmas day. She figured maybe she was overreacting about the sweater incident, but truth be told, she'd been annoyed since J.R. dropped the bomb about killing D. After they got dressed, they met up with Drea in the living room before the three of them headed next door.

"What's wrong with you?" Drea asked her baby sister, noticing the grimaced look on her face.

"Shit, I'm cool…. Just hungry," Lexi informed her.

"Hungry? All yo ass do is eat. You sure you ain't the one pregnant?" she asked, rubbing Lexi's flat stomach

"Hell yeah, I'm sure," Lexi replied, smacking her hand away.

"Yeah, I heard y'all the other night, fucking in my house," Drea said looking at J.R. that time.

"Nah, she bet not be pregnant. I'll have to kill Lexi, she'll be on that crazy baby momma shit," he joked.

"Kill me, huh? That's what you do, huh?" Lexi smirked, hoping that J.R. caught all the shade she was throwing at him.

When they entered their parents' house, the sight of breakfast being prepared made her feel better. Mrs. Holiday along with Anastasia and Aunt Shirley moved about the newly remodeled kitchen while Kyler mixed fresh blueberries inside the pancake batter.

"Merry Christmas y'all!" Alyssa yelled as her and Corey walked into the house.

"Merry Christmas!" Everyone turned towards the front door and said in unison.

"Come on, lil man," Lexi heard J.R. say to Kyler, grabbing him by the back of the head, ushering him out of the kitchen.

J.R., Corey, and Kyler went inside the living room while the Holiday ladies prepared breakfast. Once everything was done, everybody sat down and ate. It seemed as if every single person at the table stuffed their faces fast as fuck, attempting to get to the gifts that was under the tree. Lexi was no different, she couldn't wait to see the looks on everyone faces when they opened their gifts from her.

"DONE!" Kyler yelled, jumping out of his seat first and running over towards the tree.

Everyone laughed and followed his lead. Tradition in the Holiday house meant, everyone opened their gifts, from oldest to youngest and that year was no different. Drea grabbed four boxes from under the tree and passed them out to each sister.

"1...2...3," Alyssa sounded off like she did when they were kids before each sister ripped through the gold wrapping paper.

"Biiiittttccchhhhhhhh, how you know my MacBook Pro was on its last life!" Lexi screamed.

"ALEXIS.... WATCH YO MOUTH!" Mrs. Holiday warned.

"I'm sorry, ma." Lexi said followed by a light chuckle.

"Drea, these are so dope. I been wanting one for the longest," Alyssa stated.

Drea spent good money on the latest Apple MacBook Pro's that she got for her sisters.

"I love it. Thanks, sister!" Anastasia said as she walked over to the tree to grab her gifts.

"Look, y'all know I'm going through a divorce soooooo...."

"A mug, Stasia? You got us a fuckin coffee mug," Lexi blurted out before peaking around the corner to make sure her mother didn't hear.

"It's the thought that counts," Stasia laughed.

"Bitch, I don't even drink coffee," Alexis replied, causing everyone to laugh.

"I love my mug, thanks sister!" Lyssa said, buttering her up.

"Thank you. At least someone appreciates it," Anastasia replied, cutting her eyes at Lexi.

"Y'all crazy! Ok, since we opened Lyssa gift's last night, it's your turn Baby Holiday," Drea stated.

Lexi stood to her feet and went in front of the tree and cleared her throat, getting everyone's attention.

"As you can see, there is no gift from me under the tree...."

"That's not shocking," Stasia said, cutting her off.

Lexi stuck up her middle finger before continuing.

"Ever since Thanksgiving, shit... I mean, things ain't been right amongst us…"

"Shit ain't been right with y'all since birth," Aunt Shirley shouted out.

"DAMN! Can I finish, PLEASE? Ok…. Y'all made me forget where I was going with this," she said pulling out her phone.

"Aw ok, I remember now, check y'all emails," Lexi said, smiling.

"Check our emails?" Stasia repeated.

"Just do it," she replied, placing her hands on her hips.

Lexi did a silent countdown in her head and just like clockwork, all three-sister jumped up yelling. They all rushed Lexi, forming a group hug.

"What? What? What?" Aunt Shirley looked on and asked.

"Lexi paid for all of us an all-exclusive trip to Jamaica!" Drea screamed.

"Wait… Waiiittttt. I don't even have an email. How am I supposed to get my shit?" Shirley questioned.

"You ain't no Holiday sister, baby. You ain't invited," Stasia replied, dancing around in Shirley's face.

"Mommy, I have a special trip planned for you and daddy once he gets well," Alexis informed her mom who looked on smiling.

"Seeing my girls loving on each other like this is all the gift I need," Victoria said as she wiped tears away.

All four girls went and gave their mother a hug. Their embrace was interrupted by the ringing of the house phone.

"I got it," Lexi broke away and went inside the kitchen to retrieve the cordless phone.

"Merry Christmas, Daddy!" Lexi bubbled as she joined the rest of the family back in the living room.

"Let me talk to daddy." The other three pushed their way past each other to speak with him.

"Wait, I answered, so I talk first.... Go ahead, Daddy, what was you saying?"

"I just wanted to call and speak with y'all while y'all all opening gifts and everything. I know y'all will be here before they take me back for surgery, but I wanna hear all my girls' voices now," Abraham informed his youngest child.

"It's sooo good to hear your voice, daddy, and we will be there very soon. I love you." Lexi grinned, sticking out her tongue at her siblings.

"Be nice, Lexi. I love you, too. Let me speak to everybody else."

Lexi laughed because her father wasn't there, yet he knew she was doing something spiteful to her sisters. She passed Drea the phone first and from there, it went around in a circle. Lexi went over to the couch and set next to J.R., who grabbed her by the neck, pulled her close, and gave her a kiss on the cheek.

"I'm proud of you," he whispered.

"I hope so, because I'm going to need my ten stacks back since that trip was your idea."

"I got you, shorty, and I got yo gift, too. But I don't think it's appropriate to give it to you at yo people's house." J.R. told her.

Lexi wondered what it was and she felt kind of bad because with all the shit she had going on, she forgot to get him something

"Ok baby, and I'm going to give you your gift when we get back home," she replied.

"I want a baby," J.R. said, shocking the shit out of Lexi.

"You want a baby and I want a ring. I guess we both just gon be wanting shit," she responded back, causing him to laugh.

"Ok, I will see y'all at the hospital in about an hour. Kyler, Granny will be back to play with you and all your new toys," Mrs. Holiday informed her grandson before walking out the door.

Their mom left early so she could be there with their dad a little while before he went under the knife. The surgery could take anywhere between one to three hours. Once Kyler opened his gifts, they were going to head that way, too. For the next thirty minutes, the girls sat around and talked while J.R. and Corey helped Kyler put his train set together. Lexi excused herself from her sisters and went onto the front porch to smoke a blunt. Not long after being out there, J.R., Corey, and Shirley joined in on the smoke session. For it to be December, the weather was beautiful, it had to at least be almost sixty degrees. Alexis closed her eyes and allowed the smoke to fill her lungs while the cool breeze crept under her sweater.

"Who that pulling up in that Beamer," Lexi heard J.R. ask.

She popped open her eyes just in time to see Richard getting out the car and storming towards them.

"That's Stasia's bitch ass husband," Aunt Shirley replied, taking a hard pull from the blunt.

"Anastasia, yo bitch ass husband out here," Lexi cracked opened the front door and yelled.

Richard came onto the porch looking like he was out for blood. He wore a pair of gray jogging pants and a Champion hoodie that was two sizes too small. Lexi moved in front of the door, guarding it because she knew that's where he was headed.

"MOVE!" he yelled into her face.

"It's excuse me," Lexi snapped, rolling her neck.

"It's get the fuck out my way," Richard snapped back.

"Hold on, buddy. You got me fucked up," J.R. said, grabbing Richard by the back of his neck, damn near tossing him out of Alexis's face.

Richard stumbled, falling onto Corey, who pushed his ass onto the ground.

"What the fuck is going on out here?" Stasia asked, finally coming out the house.

"Aye yo, sis, I'm about to pop yo husband if he don't chill out," J.R. informed Stasia.

"Do yo thang bro," Stasia smirked, folding her arms across her chest.

"I'm going to ignore your hoodlum ass cousin because I came here for a more important reason. Where the fuck is my son?" Richard fumed.

"Richard, get the fuck on somewhere. My son is fine and now that I think about it, he ain't ask about yo tired ass not once," she said matter-of-factly.

"You taking him away from me is kidnapping and -."

"SHUT UP, BITCH! SHE CAN'T KIDNAPP HER OWN SON DUMMY!" Aunt Shirley stated, causing everyone, but Richard to laugh.

Richard looked at Shirley and rolled his eyes like a little girl.

"As I was saying…." He tried to continue, but was silenced by Drea and Lyssa running out the house screaming.

"I just got a call from mom, dad went into cardiac arrest, they don't think he gon' make it."

Everyone one on the porch ran to their respective cars and headed to the hospital with hopes on what they just heard not being true.

Chapter 30

Anastasia and her sisters rushed out of the house and straight to Alyssa's truck with tears streaming down all of their faces. The last thing they had expected to hear was that something was wrong with their father. As she hopped into the front seat with Alyssa behind the wheel, Anastasia wiped the tears from her eyes, but they kept coming, and she could hear both Alexis and Drea in the backseat breaking down. The only one who seemed to be keeping their cool was Alyssa, because although she was crying, she was still able to maneuver them to the hospital. Anastasia figured it came with the territory of being a Fed, but at that moment, she was glad that somebody was level headed. All that ran through Stasia's mind was how her and her sister's petty beef had been the reason for him even going through all of the illnesses. It seemed like just when things were starting to look good for the sisters, something else came and threatened their newfound bonds. She could hear Alexis in the backseat trying to calm Andrea down, so that she didn't stress out the twins, and more tears slipped from her eyes. Sure, Anastasia and her father had their moments, but she loved him and knew that she wanted him to be okay.

Alyssa pulled up to the hospital damn near on two wheels and Stasia held on for dear life as she watched her sister park her big ass truck. Once they parked, everyone stepped out and Anastasia reached for her sister's hands. She stood in between Alexis and Andrea while Alyssa stood on the other side of Drea. They walked inside holding hands and climbed into the first elevator that was available.

"Y'all I swear I don't know what I'm gonna do if something happens to daddy," Drea wailed, pacing the small space.

The look of worry and dread on her face made Anastasia even more worried about their father's condition. That time Alyssa went and attempted to console her.

"Please, I know you're worried Drea, but I don't want you stressing the babies out. Daddy will be just fine. What did he tell us to do in times of fear?" she asked, her voice getting stronger as she spoke.

"To pray," They all mumbled in unison, bringing a small smile to Drea's worried face.

"That's right, and that's exactly what we're gonna do," Alyssa told them with a nod as the doors dinged open.

"Be strong y'all."

They all walked off of the elevator together still crying silently, but saying their own personal prayers. They were damn near running to see what was going on with their father as fear gripped them all. As they got closer to his room they could hear yelling and it sounded like their Aunt Shirley.

"I don't give a damn, Victoria! You should have been told that girl!" she screamed at her sister while Stasia heard her mother crying.

"Don't you stand there and tell me what I should have done, Shirley! There was never a reason for her to know any of this shit!" her mother yelled back and Anastasia's eyes bucked in surprise. Their mother never cursed unless she was extremely upset.

"She has lived her entire life trying to please y'all and doing everything she can to make y'all proud! The very least you could have done was tell her the truth! Andrea deserves to know!"

"Do you think that somebody can just come right out and tell their child that the only father they've ever known isn't really hers? How could I tell her that the man she's called Daddy all these years isn't? Huh?"

The sister's stopped just behind Andrea as she opened the door on that last bit of information, and immediately her back stiffened. Their mother and Aunt Shirley stopped their heated argument and their eyes landed on her, but she still didn't move or say anything.

"Andrea," Their mother tried to talk, but she clearly seemed at a loss for words.

"He's not my daddy?" she asked in a meek voice, still not walking into the room any further.

"Listen to me honey..."

"No! Are you saying that... that my daddy isn't MY DADDY?!" she demanded as tears rushed down her face.

Alexis stood back with her hand over her mouth shaking at the revelation while Alyssa held her and whispered comforting words into her ear. Stasia too wrapped her arms around her big sister trying to console her and ease her back out of the room.

"Is daddy dead?" Alexis wanted to know, drawing all eyes to the bed. Their father lay under a white sheet with his face covered.

"And you didn't even call to say that he had died, Ma! Was y'all that busy in here arguing that y'all failed to call and tell us that our father was dead!" Drea shrieked wildly.

"Andrea please... just calm down," their mother said, hoping that her daughter would give her a chance to explain.

"Is... the daddy I've known all my life... not my daddy?" Andrea asked again and that time instead of saying anything, her mother merely shook her head no.

Anastasia and her sisters stood quietly still crying until she confirmed their fears and they all shrieked in shock.

"What?"

"Oh, my God, Ma!"

"Are you serious?"

They all shouted at the same time looking at their mother in confusion. The very last thing they expected to hear was that their oldest sister didn't share a father with them. Their mother stood off to the side silently crying while Andrea ran out of the room. Anastasia and Alyssa were too shocked to move, but Lexi ran after her.

Chapter 31

Drea took off running with no particular destination in mind. Her eyes were blurry and burning as tears continued to stream down her face. She just couldn't believe the news that she heard. It felt like her whole life turned upside down in the blink of an eye. Her whole life had been a lie. How could her parents keep such a deep, dark secret like that? Drea heard her mom saying something, but she couldn't stop. She needed to get away. As soon as she got to the elevator, she fumbled with buttons until it finally opened. When she stepped on, someone grabbed her.

"We gonna get through this sister," Lexi comforted her.

No words came out of Drea's mouth, only uncontrollable sobs. Lexi pulled her closer and squeezed her tight. They stood there for what seemed like an eternity with Drea's cries being the only noise that was heard. A few minutes later, her phone started ringing. She wasn't in the mood to talk to anyone, but Lexi grabbed her phone and answered after the first call ended and it rang again.

"Hey brother-in-law... my sister needs you... we lost our dad... and some other stuff... yeah... University of Mississippi Medical Center... straight down Lakeland to State Street... okay, bye."

She halfway listened as Lexi talked to who had to be D, since she called him her brother-in-law at the beginning of the call. Lexi reached over and hit the button to go to the first floor. Right before the doors closed, J.R. appeared and got on the elevator. Drea tried her best to get herself together. She knew that she had to be strong no matter what, and that was exactly what she was going to do. Everyone always depended on her and she couldn't let them down despite the circumstances. Even with the news that they had just heard, Abraham was still her daddy, no matter what. He was all that she knew. Abraham Holiday had his ways, as all parents do, but they loved him in spite of. It was crazy how they all had just talked to him and then, boom. Life sure was funny. The lawyer side of her wanted answers, while the soft side of her just wanted the entire day to be a dream that she could wake up from instantly.

"I don't even know what to say to y'all... but, I do know that the love that y'all have been showing this past week has been real. Y'all gotta keep that goin and move forward," J.R. advised.

"He's right, Drea... on the way over last week he was telling me that we gotta stick together no matter what. All families go through bullshit, but we fuckin Holidays and we gon get through this... TOGETHER!!"

"Thanks y'all! Both of y'all are absolutely right!" Drea finally found her voice.

"I just need some air... let's go outside for a while please."

When the elevator chimed, Drea stepped off first. She saw a sign for a bathroom and told Lexi and J.R. that she was going to get herself together for a minute.

"You need me to go wit you sister?"

"Nah, I'm good Baby Holiday. I'll be right back. I just need to get myself together right quick."

Drea made her way to the restroom. Thankfully, no one was inside, so she really had a moment to herself. She stared into the mirror and wondered what God's reasoning for the chain of events that had just transpired could have been. Things had been going to great, only to take such a drastic turn for the worse. On Christmas Day at that. Drea loved her family dearly, but she was actually happy that Lexi had told D to come to the hospital. There was something about a male companion that made things a little better during hard times. Drea hadn't had that in almost never, so she appreciated D. She had no idea what it was they were doing, but everything about him and the situation felt so right. She wanted to feel his strong arms wrapped around her.

After she cleaned her face, she noticed that her eyes were still red and puffy, but there wasn't anything that she could do about it. They would probably be that way for days to come. Drea made her way back out and she saw Lexi and J.R. standing near the door. When she walked up, Lexi gave her another hug, and then they walked outside. It was December, and the Christmas season had officially started three days ago, but the sun was shining and it was fifty-five degrees. The light coats they had on was all that they needed.

"There go ya maannn!" Lexi sang.

As soon as she said it, Drea looked to her left and saw D headed her way. The swag that he had was out of the world. No one could even blame Drea for sleeping with him and getting pregnant on the first night. He came up to her and grabbed her and pulled her into his arms. Just like before, his cologne hit her nostrils and drew her in further. Even though she had told herself that she was going to be strong, as soon as she was deep in his arms, Drea's tears started back.

"I got you, ma… I promise I got you!" He squeezed her tight.

He comforted her and everything was alright, if only for the moment. Out of nowhere, Drea heard her sister's voice and it wasn't pleasant.

"What the fuck is going on?" Anastasia yelled.

"Stasia, what the fuck wrong wit you?" Lexi stepped to her as soon as Drea turned around.

"Move Lexi! Get outta my way!"

"First, you wit a random ass bitch and now you hugged up wit my sister!!" Stasia fumed.

"What the fuck you talking bout?" D queried.

"I'm sick of you playing me to the left like I'm some random ass bitch. Just because I couldn't leave when you asked, you play me to the left while I'm going through a divorce!"

Drea couldn't believe what she was hearing. Was D her sister's lover? As if everything that had happened wasn't already enough, it appeared that more had just been added.

"So, you really thought that this thug could replace me? Look at you standing there looking just like the stupid bitch that you are!" Richard walked up and said.

Before anyone could say another word, J.R. made his way to Richard and punched him in the face. Richard fell straight to the ground as blood splattered from his nose and he screamed like a bitch. D removed himself away from Drea and went and gave Richard another blow that caused him to lay all the way out on the concrete.

"Don't disrespect women you punk ass nigga!" D spat.

"What the fuck you think you doin, nigga?" Anastasia stepped to him and pushed him upside the head.

"Look, lil mama... I don't even..."

"D'Mani, Ima fuck you up if you keep acting like you don't know me," Stasia yelled and pushed him.

"Stasia!! Keep ya damn hands to ya self!" a voice rang out from behind.

Drea turned around and couldn't believe her eyes. D had told her that he had a brother, but he failed to mention that he had a twin brother.

"Oh my God... what the hell?" Stasia said and covered her mouth with both hands.

"I don't know what my brother did to you, but I ain't him... I'm D'Mari, but everybody calls me D."

To Be Continued...

Thug Holiday 3 will be released on Valentine's Day 2018

CPSIA information can be obtained
at www.ICGtesting.com
Printed in the USA
LVHW01s1630140518
577119LV00013B/1291/P